ONCE INTO THE NIGHT

ONCE INTO THE NIGHT

AURELIE SHEEHAN

TUSCALOOSA

FC2 is an imprint of The University of Alabama Press
Inquiries about reproducing material from this work should be addressed
to The University of Alabama Press

Book Design: Publications Unit, Department of English, Illinois State
    University; Director: Steve Halle, Production Intern: Ben Sutton
Cover Design: Lou Robinson
Typeface: Baskerville

Library of Congress Cataloging-in-Publication Data

Names: Sheehan, Aurelie, author.
Title: Once into the night / Aurelie Sheehan.
Description: Tuscaloosa : FC2, [2019]
Identifiers: LCCN 2018042587 (print) | LCCN 2018045916 (ebook) |
ISBN
  9781573668811 (E-book) | ISBN 9781573660716 (pbk.)
Classification: LCC PS3569.H392155 (ebook) | LCC PS3569.H392155
A6 2019
  (print) | DDC 813/.54—dc23
LC record available at https://lccn.loc.gov/2018042587

For Reed and Zaza

CONTENTS

FOREWORD

LAIRD HUNT

Deep in this wonderful collection, near the middle of a very short piece called "Writer," Aurelie Sheehan's narrator speaks of "junky glory," and it is tempting, having signaled this coinage of an expression that so succinctly sums up the early twenty-first century American dispensation, to simply drop the metaphorical mic (on Sheehan's behalf) and get the heck out of the way. So tempting that even as I continue—for the form insists—I invite you to leap immediately ahead into a world of compressed and raucous wonder. There you will find stories short and shorter in which the darkness sparks and crackles and heaves and howls and sighs. Light, when it is mentioned, is likely to come from "the turn of the earth, from planets colliding three trillion light years away, from a pebble turning under a collision of storms. . . ."

Everywhere the stakes are very high and very real in Sheehan's work. On the first page, a character is busy being "born [on a bench] in the swift of the night," and on the last, another sneaks out the back door of a nursing home with a friend, flies to Paris, and listens to Edith Piaf and Duke Ellington "until we both nodded off at last, completely dead."

If you are still here, or are back from a sojourn in Sheehan's wordscapes I'll wager was difficult to curtail, let me note that truth, rage, tenderness, boredom, beauty, sadness, and weirdness lock arms and press palms (as closely as they can) with great intricacy and refreshing candor on these pages. Indeed, I thought more than once as I read of one of those amazing skeleton watches that remain fully legible even as they show you the complexity of their movement, all the screws and gears that move together to make their meaning fully on display. Sometimes sheer sound makes *Once into the Night*'s gears engage. "I have just turned my back on a stray cat, betrayed by her lank shank, the subterfuge in her approach, her softness." Elsewhere, clear-eyed world-organizing perception holds sway. "The suit I wore for so many days in a row was comprised of a slim skirt and a short boxy jacket with half sleeves and one large mother-of-pearl button at the neck. The important thing about the suit is that it clung and held, trimming you up and making sure you were all in one place, headed in the right direction. You couldn't actually move your arms that much. You couldn't reach too far for things."

But this book can and does. Sheehan is a spelunker, always taking the deep drop, getting right to it, shining her torch on crud and fabulous crystal alike. "All those splintered boards, spiraling down into emptiness, and then the wrecking waters." Junky glory, indeed. Spines meander in *Once into the Night*. Crows come to roost. Hippos congregate in the flower garden. Teeth sink into tiny cars. A wolf called "Wolfie" is kept in the basement. "Darkness was a dust storm to make our way through. . . ."

Everywhere in *Once into the Night* a charged, fraught, *hard-won* intimacy presides. Turn these pages and you will learn things that won't leave you. Did you know, for example, "that when humans are touching there is a $1/250$ of an inch separating them, always?" It is in that space that great engines of steam and breath and life collide.

ONCE INTO THE NIGHT

ORIGIN

I was born on a bench in a park in a small country. Everyone knew each other back then, in that place. I was born in the swift of night, however, and to be honest they weren't completely sure I'd been *born* on the bench—but it was on the bench I was found by them, the warm people of that small country.

WOLF IN THE BASEMENT

When I was young, we kept a wolf in the basement. It was a compromise, where one of my parents wanted no wolf and the other wanted the wolf in the living room, and so together they came up with this solution. The wolf lived six steps down from the rest of us, and when we let him out it was from the very back door, the one that faced the forest.

At first I did not like the wolf. I was a cat person. And we already had a cat—a longhaired, skinny thing, at times willing to let you touch her. When I did pet Minerva, she gave me a look like, *this is niceish, probably more so for you than me.* I twirled my fingers under her creamy chin, ran them down her gray back.

So would the wolf eat my cat? If the door unlatched and what was upstairs went downstairs or vice versa?

We found the wolf one afternoon on the grounds of an old mansion where we'd gone for a book sale, proceeds of which would go to my mother's alma mater. We went to this event every year, filling boxes with volumes that cost dimes or quarters. Neither of my parents was profligate, and so the outing always had a feeling of splendor. In the capacious blank rooms, winding lines of books—whole paragraphs of them.

Our boxes were already in the back of the car, and my mother stood off to the side, having a smoke—her arms in an L, like a military hand signal, cigarette wavering in the vicinity of her mouth. She paused, sightline going from middle distance to zoned-in. "Larry?"

Dad was still arranging the boxes for transport, I guess, because he was at this point half tumbled into the back of the car. He got up, hit his head on the car roof, pushed the hatch door down with a solid thwack. "*What?*" No answer, but my mother's aura of concentration compelled him to walk over to where she stood. I followed, as did my brother (walking like a clown, as per usual). The four of us stared past a small precipice at the wolf, sitting forlornly near a pine tree where he might have been viewing the book fair but was now, most definitely, gazing at us. He got up, limped two steps, and sat down again, all the while keeping up his plaintive look.

"Wow, a wolf!" I said.

"A wolf, Mommy!" said my brother.

"It looks injured," muttered my father.

"Let's go see if we can help," said my mother, a maniacal gleam in her eye. She tossed the cigarette.

We lived in a town well known for its crafty, can-do spirit. It was a survivalist town, filled with melancholy people, and the sky above was mostly white. In that town and in those years, I saw the sky as a sequence of key shapes. This key, that key, skeleton keys, Medeco keys. Sometimes jumbles, sometimes singular. It was all very intricate, I felt, in my prolonged, or even endless, it can seem now, study.

However, none of us really did have the key, so to speak, or the keys were always soft and amorphous and not ready for one little hole or secret. We labored along in our crafty survivalist lives, performing the act of a family. It wasn't just an act—of course not. We *were* a family. And yet as with every family, while there was a tension or magnetic force keeping us close, there was an equal yearning or leaning, like a Shetland pony on a rope, away from the centripetal field.

I was in charge of bringing the wolf his vittles. I used a plastic measuring cup to get his portion out of the garbage can where we ended up keeping the "dog" food, a receptacle until recently used for near-the-laundry trash, fluffs of dryer lint mostly, carrying it downstairs into the dark, wolf-bearing basement. (We'd tried storing the food in the basement, but he'd handily knocked over the can and gorged himself.) I turned on the light at the top of the stairs. We kept the wolf in the dark, although during the day some light did come in the back door. And of course when my father took him jogging he saw the light, or when my mother, alone in the house, let him out at twelve and three, into the backyard. We'd called our vet soon after we first lured him into our hatchback—a wolf among the books—but our vet, a sanctimonious Catholic, had cautioned us that wolves were illegal, and so if he were really a wolf, we'd need to *turn him in.* (Turn him into what, or whom?) In any case he himself, God-fearing, etc., refused to treat the wolf. My mother and father did agree, at that moment, on the asshole- ness of that veterinarian.

We ended up using a sketchy vet from Norwalk—he need- ed the work.

I flipped the light switch, and this is what I saw: the washer and dryer, a linen chest, an old dresser filled with art and random objects, the pool filter and pump, stored patio furniture, an an- cient gray-green carpet. In the middle of the carpet lay Wolfie, his head angled tragically on his now-healed front paw. He jumped up and stood whenever I appeared, half embarrassed, it seemed, to be caught unaware, or in sorrow. Oh, Wolfie—but ours was a stoic town, and we envisioned ourselves as stoic people.

I put the bowl down and watched expressionlessly as he padded toward the food. He was small for a wolf, and even weeks after his capture he still had a bit of a limp. He was a black wolf, which is unusual I've been told. Perhaps he was a Russian wolf. He would have looked good in the snow, in a snowy field. I went back upstairs, to the crunch of vittles.

One day about four months later—after school ended anyway, because I was waking up late (the sky a brighter white than on school mornings)—I looked out the window and saw Wolfie and Minerva both free in the yard.

The wolf and the cat were staring at each other. Wolfie lunged, his body blurring into an italic, and Minerva lunged too, becoming more of a dash. Within two seconds Wolfie was barking at the chain-link fence and Minerva stood on the other side, tail bristled out, looking at him with scandal and dull horror.

Some mornings I watched as my father and Wolfie walked down the driveway on their way out for a run, my father's bright blue running shorts like an Olympic sprinter's, and Wolfie with his patient padding paws, and the white sky overhead, and the crunch of gravel.

My father would soon be gone, but for what seemed like forever he was right there, in the driveway or in the kitchen or in his office (also in the basement, a small room off the central area). Both parents gave up smoking, and I started smoking. At Thanksgiving, we set aside some dark meat for the wolf. Plans were hatched, grades were dispensed, fights were had up and downstairs. My brother became excellent at sports. We lost some, but not all of our relatives.

On the last day my father ran with the wolf—it was an early summer evening—I turned away from the window and sat on my bed. My room was a box lined with Laura Ashley wallpaper and decorated with one peacock feather. Minerva declined my invitation to be petted. My mother was downstairs doing something inscrutable. My brother was at baseball practice.

We all escaped that town eventually, even Wolfie.

Still his shape remains with me, his shape like a shadow or an outline or someone's scribble. I remember his grieving face when we first saw him, sitting at the edge of the field by the old mansion, with all the people buying books very near, getting back into their Datsuns and Peugeot wagons, and the tranquil way he let us take him—meaning, said the sketchy Norwalk vet, that he was very under the weather indeed. He got better and better in our basement, and as he got better he must have realized where he was, didn't he? I remember bringing him his portion of food, and I remember his moments of freedom— his mysterious runs with my father, the foreshortened hunt involving Minerva or the occasional squirrel. Some days I'd see him padding around the edge of the yard along the chain-link fence. Then he'd lie down, staring with his black eyes in his black face under the white sky.

I was growing up, I guess. So was my brother.

In the afternoons I sat on the stairs between the first floor, where Minerva lay unmolested, and the basement, where Wolfie slept close to the door. His fur did not shine. Some hours, he slept with his eyes open. The light from the door came in brief streaks and squares, easily dissuaded. Darkness was a dust storm to make our way through, a forest road to run down.

SEA TRAVEL

I spent my early adulthood at sea. I even had a boat—or my boyfriend did, but we lived together, and he was generous in sharing his things. The term "early adulthood" is a patch of gray laid over whatever those years were, however long they lasted. Now I'm in "adulthood," another magazine column category.

Here is what I thought of love. *Love*, def.: *doing things with, having a similar sense of humor as, extracting a future in addition to.*

The sea was a vivid black, folds of black relentlessly and unpredictably overlapping. Its opaqueness came from how the sun hit the water, or from the swallowing of the moon. You simply couldn't see. I couldn't see, anyway.

Life was long; it was a bit cheap and certainly plentiful—maybe even too long, a great amount of this one capacious thing, like a basket of yarn crushed and laced together, mixed-up and knotted and not yielding.

We brought sandwiches on the boat with us, or sometimes a thermos of soup. If we were traveling some distance I was obliged to pee in a bucket. Afterward, he would lie on the deck and drop the bucket down on its rope and the seawater cleaned out the interior. We liked pecan sandies for dessert.

When we were in the long process of breaking up, yet still grocery shopping together on Sundays, we were confused about what to buy—unsure if we would be together for the whole week. Should we buy our typical meals, our favorite items? Should we buy misery food, or just very, very plain food, rations, no salt or sauce? It was a package of pecan sandies that made us feel the saddest on one of those grocery runs, back in early adulthood.

Sometimes on the boat I stared at the horizon—this was even before the weeks and months of tearing apart. Something already felt sad in the world. Perhaps it was the sea itself, the difference between the opaque surface and the steely gravity underneath. Perhaps it was my inability to distinguish between having a vast basket of yarn and having just a little yarn left.

I wish I could tell you of our travels. Some of the places we went were fancy, and we dressed in vintage clothing and acted like Gatsby, drinking more than the average adult. There was no end to the places that smelled deeply, richly of pine. Pine by the sea, pine in the heart of ancient forests, pine a perfume passed through on our hurried way to the shore or back up from the shore, *it was there for you.*

SARA APPLEWOOD

I.

I am hitting Sara Applewood. I hit her on the shoulders and back after she has fallen on the ski slope. *Get up, get up, get up, Sara.* The world is vast and ornamental and also small, winnowed down to the point of contact where my pole hits her back, not doing enough damage through the parka, hence moving up to the head and shoulders. She holds her arm up so she won't be hurt. People are looking, as at a grocery store if there's been a spill. I don't want my mother to look. I don't want anyone to say: *Stop it, little girl.* I keep hitting for a while, getting a last good one in, and then I adjust my mitten and the pole strap, bend my knees, and push off. It's a small rise on a large mountain, and I slide down and around, skiing to the middle of the whiteness where there are hardly any people, the wide white middle, where I spy an invisible trail.

II.

Sara Applewood is hitting me. She's wearing her sleek red parka with lift passes on the zipper from places professional skiers go, Swiss slopes visited with her parents and governess. My God, a governess! But that's life for Sara Applewood, sadist and betrayer. Ski slopes are like heaven, except for when you're down on the ground being beaten. She really does enjoy hurting others—but who could possibly enjoy that? I'm a pacifist, an animal lover, and a non-litterer, except there have been those times when I've held my brother down to the point where I thought a bone might break, or once when I threatened him with a knife (a butter knife). Was that pleasure? Sara Applewood has always been a better athlete than me. Her calves are hard and her toes grip the floor like an ape's. She has a sway to her back, her butt sticks out, and she pushes out her chest too. *See?* she's always saying. *See me now?* The world is cold as a sheet of metal, and I'm a slumped, Goodwill-bedecked lump—except for in my stomach, right in the center of my body, is a bit of warmth, a dull unfolding. Another hit off my shoulder, another on my sleeve. Then she's skiing away, her bitchy braids flying out behind her as she disappears, slaloming down the slope alone. The sun has slipped behind the mountain. The big gleaming mirror of cold—it's nothing, it's containable, blink and it's gone. I put my pole in the snow and push. *Swash*, goes my pole, again and again. Defeat almost has me. "Sara!" I shout, "Sara Applewood!" Hate is a bunny in my belly.

SEX WORKER

I am a sex worker, and it's a good gig, because the bawdy room is everywhere.

I slice pickles for sandwiches and the tense guests await this enactment and then I enact something else, tilting my body so they can see the full, one hundred percent posterboard of who I am. "These sliced pickles might be excellent on your sandwich," I say, moving forward with the platter. It's a descent from the sky, my parachute emanating from behind. My face is large and wide, and then you're taking a camera ride into my mouth, sliding along my tongue, clutched by my throat, and on and on and deeper. I can do one person at a time, but it's especially nerve-racking and advantageous if there's a group around the table, ideally relatives.

Sex is multidimensional. I don't want to be patronizing, but people don't understand how multidimensional we're talking.

At the stoplight. At Target. During the flossing ritual. With insects.

I'm very tired of late.

But let me start at the beginning of my career. I was naked in my room with the blue shag carpet, standing before the full-length mirror. I saw it—an invitation, an opportunity. This body, as it turned out, was built for something, as a rocket is built to propel into space. It was a job, and the tools were handy.

I launched myself, stealthily draped, into the world. The town center was small, buildings made of brick with white doors. Tentative at first, I took big slow steps. At the grocery store I bought a plum and a pack of cigarettes. I stood in the dimension and geometry of sun and shade by the liquor store. Men who were like my father but were not my father spoke in boisterous and ritualized tones. Other men sat in passenger seats, in idling trucks, staring forward.

Must we be paid? I don't know about that, but some of my greatest working moments have been at least social in nature. There was the time the man flung himself upon my car. His look through the windshield at me, a lady with her hands on the wheel, a pink blazer. My look through the windshield at him, one cheek smashed up against glass, a comrade or a customer, pretty willing to go to another bar.

* * *

It's Saturday. I take off my clothes and lay on a pile of sheets, a big heap of what I could find in the linen closet. I stretch my arms up and over in a dolphin curve; I scissor my legs in slow motion. I don't put on music. I'm already attending to the music of the day: a dove cooing, a police siren, a glimmer of wind, even a neighbor getting into a car. There's a connection between my naked self and these sounds. At times I sense I'm too low . . . I might be better off on a bier or perch. I'm a little landlocked, swiveling here on the floor. Nonetheless I wrap myself in the variously hued sheets, and wait for sounds to pass through the cloth to my ears.

Sometimes there is a grid element to sex work. Laying myself on the day, I'm an elemental formation, a cloud, and all the particulars of my body become the vastness of time and geography.

Sometimes in a social moment, I have sat with another person in a tent and marked the lines on our bodies, matching the lines together in private triangles and squares. Our blood pumped and coursed, as if we ourselves were planets with obedient rivers.

When I was young and the men hung around the liquor store, and some had already gone in, and some were going in later, I passed through their bodies, too, as if they were made of netting, as if all the people were their own grids, and I was just wind, or the noon siren from the fire station, or the smell of lavender.

THE SUIT

I wore a particular '50s-style suit for almost a year when I was in graduate school. I realized what was going on one afternoon when I was standing in the English Department's mailroom. I was a graduate assistant at the time. A man who had the name of another man was in the room with me, getting his mail. Soon he would die. He was loved and appreciated at that school, though he worked for limited and unfair pay (the adjunct scale). I chose to wear the suit because there was a scale, and on one side was success and allure and affect, and on the other side was rumpled-ness and sorrow and suicide. The suit I wore was my mother's wedding suit. She wore a suit, rather than a white dress, that singular day. The wedding took place on the army base in Fort Dix, New Jersey, and I was in her belly already, a firmament of my own behind the still-flat skirt panel, behind the small bouquet. She also wore a hat. Her mother was there at the wedding, and her mother was also wearing a suit and a hat. The suit I wore for so many days in a row was comprised of a slim skirt and a short boxy jacket with half sleeves and one large mother-of-pearl button at the neck. The important thing about the suit is that it clung and held, trimming you up and making sure you were all in one place, headed in the right direction. You couldn't actually move your arms that much. You couldn't reach too far for things. And of course you couldn't walk forward with great strides, either, but needed to almost shuffle forward. High heels were best, obviously, or little Chinese slippers (created a nice sound with the shuffling). Hard to find the right blouse to go underneath (not too billowy) or the exact right hairstyle (something contrasting, but also coiffed), but if you got those things right you could pretty much remain in neutral and feel satisfied.

In those days I also slept in the suit, in a coffin. Actually it wasn't a coffin, but a single bed with a thin mattress and very high sides, so I did have to stumble in, straining the suit as I flipped myself into the horizontal resting place. I held my arms to my body. I didn't wear shoes, but kept my shoes (pumps or flats) on the floor at the foot of the bed. Sleep wasn't always as restful as it could have been.

ART MOVIE

The celluloid is burnt and bubbled, creased in places, all imperfections flattened out and digitized. It is us, mother and daughter, *entre nous*. Snow, mud. Night is falling. The distance between our heights, the angle of our arms. We are walking on the side of a snowy field, before a hedgerow. You are a Russian peasant princess, a heroine. I feel the cold between my snowsuit sleeve and my mitten. I rely on you.

The film has changed, the reels run together; still we roll forward. I could put music to this spliced-up compendium. You say: *Tell it to me now, so you don't need to write about it later.* What is there to tell? *Tell me about your childhood.*

ENNUI

I had been filled with ennui all week. It was drenching, and all I could do was walk around, taking furtive looks at things, being alone with myself and my ennui. It's a surprising shadow, ennui is, or a cockroach in a Snickers wrapper, or the end of the play when everyone takes off their costumes. I furrow my brow at these things—in slight, but recoverable, disarray.

In my regular life, when not felled by ennui, I paint pictures of trees in various attitudes, almost like the stages of life—not the historical ascension stages, from creepy ape to upright '50s man, but the personal path: ball of baby, spry youth, productive citizen, laughable old person with cane, grim-reaper invisibility. I would say most of my paintings are of trees without leaves.

Still and all, it didn't seem like enough, and last night the ennui finally overcame me. Before I knew it, I had swallowed the entire house. I lay right down on the bed, as if I'd been shot. I was splayed on my back (can't lie on your stomach after eating a house). I burped. I stared at the ceiling. What was this like, I asked myself, feeling, at least, analytical. My eyes stung and I could no longer see the lines of the beams. I could hear, like a faded dream, my family speaking in the living room. One person spoke; the other person spoke. Silences occurred. *When they leave me, I will be alone.* But at least I'll have swallowed the house, I thought, cackling in the bedroom.

MY INVISIBLE TATTOOS

I have a tattoo over my left shoulder, a circle within a circle, and if I'm at my desk or watching a bird at the birdfeeder, it remains so, two perfect circles. The larger one is a black outline with purple fenestration inside, like ivy or something melting. The interior circle is red. I also have a tattoo in the "tramp stamp" area. Mine is of a hand, the hand of a nun, or perhaps the hand of a saint, or it could be the hand of a dead person. The hand is severed at the wrist, or just halts, as if the painter paused and might come back at another time. The fingers are narrow and almost bony, in repose, or perhaps a slight gesture toward. They have no rings on them or marks of any kind. I have a tattoo behind my ear of a bird seen from behind—a bird butt if you like, but it looks like a flower, a chrysanthemum. The bird is on its way into my body, I think, but he will not stay. His speedy flying is apparent, as if he's already almost gone. I have a tattoo on the bottom of my foot: a knife. In the airport I unfurl my sock and sit down on a bright plastic chair, stretch my foot out to the man in the uniform. He looks at me sadly. I would like it if he touched the blade, tried to determine the reality of the situation. I have a blanket tattoo, which some have mistaken for a toga. I get a little tired of explaining that one. It's not a toga; it's not some prop in a Latin play. It's a blanket of words, fallen in dishabille. You can read words, but it's impossible to make out a complete sentence, for the folds disappear into my skin. The closest is: "The water in her glass reflected some of the winter's . . ." which is not meant to be a symbol for anything, not a statement of intent. The insects all over my hands and arms you can see, of course, the scattering of bugs and spiders and butterflies, the resplendent fruit and leaves that hold them. There is a block of green and black over my hip, which can now be seen as a clasp, perhaps, for the blanket of words, but was not originally that. It is a careful box that has something in it, and which holds something back.

FROM THE AIR

I grew up in a dull place. It would have been better if there was more desolation, shadowed cliffs or holes where I'd be walking walking walking and then—*whoof!*—everything gone. But no, I woke every morning to the same. Fell asleep, the same. I tried to liven things up a bit. I sewed hearts on my boobs and butt and hitchhiked everywhere: to school, to the glen, to Westport. It was disappointing that brushes with adventure seemed largely to feature men of uncertain moral standing and less certain hygiene. My parents were troublesome, but not troublesome enough. My friend's parents got closer to the ideal. Sometimes one of the Porsches would end up parked mysteriously on the side of the highway; in the morning someone would need to go pick it up. Crossing the median. Laughing convulsively. Later: cocaine, bongs, and glitter-eyed women in Danskin wraps. So there was that. If no cars stopped for me, at some point the distance between where I'd been and where I wanted to go reached the tipping point, and I turned around and walked. Each step forward took me a tiny, tiny distance, the kind of distance you can't even see from overhead. School was absurd, there was nothing to be found there, not in conversation with teachers, not in class, not by reading their books. I had a dream I was at a stressful country-collapsing-under-siege airport, blue button-down blouse, baby in my arms.

SILENCE

The sobering thing is to remember the times I remained silent, sitting in my chair, or when I made a certain hand gesture or facial expression: *I will acquiesce to your statement.* Or when in some fever instead I argued a point that was not the point at all, but another point. I have never, really, tried to lie—except for a couple of paltry times, and then a few other rather more significant ones. Granted, I've forged whole friendships with lies. I stand here and present myself to you, then furtively sniff this paste. I stand here and present myself to you, blowing smoke in this sophisticated manner. I will sleep with you or I won't sleep with you—purely arbitrary. How can a fuck be a lie? Well, let me explain.

MY MOTHER'S IDEAS

I am lying on my back, hoping they won't ask me to do another downward dog. *You are beautiful just the way you are.* "And now it's time for an inversion," says the lithe instructor. At a party the other night I was regaling someone with the (exciting) story of how I do like yoga now but I'm pretty inflexible—inflexible *physically*, I added, implying my flexibility of spirit—and this kind and urgent person said, "Do this," and she held her arms out to both sides of her body, as if about to give a hug. I did the same. She said, "You are flexible. You're fine." I said, "Oh, okay." I felt like she really might hug me.

Part of the problem, if it is a problem, which the instructor would say it is not, is that my spine meanders from my coccyx to my skull, rather than taking the more traditional straight path. When I was eleven and had just begun wearing a brace, the orthopedist suggested a series of daily exercises. His nurse gave us a photocopied set of instructions. The drawings depicted a young person with mild features and an overall demeanor of acquiescence. My mother sat next to me in the living room, though I didn't really need help with the exercises, bland as the illustrations. Five, eight, fifteen reps. Floor lint. Cat fur. Augmenting Western medicine and everyone a little panicked as my curves got worse, my mother brought me to my first yoga class a few months later. It was 1975, when yoga was vaguely, suburbanly counterculture.

Surrounded by middle-aged women in my mother's friend's living room, I om-ed, did a Salutation to the Sun or two, and fell asleep during meditation. Was it working; was I being healed? This was always the question. Much evidence to the contrary, but my mother persevered. She suggested I dialogue with my back. "Your spine can speak to you," she explained as we sat on the sofa. Her voice was soft, enticing. I could fall into the murmuring well of her ideas.

I put the yoga brick under my coccyx. *Hey back, are you okay?* I think to myself, legs up in the air—a dialogue, indeed. The dissonance between what I wanted to do and what I felt I should do to please my mother. The inability to say no in any concrete way. A kind of terror of this. Fucking up yoga.

"Put space between things, that's what we're doing," says the yoga instructor. Time to lie down again. I remove the brick from underneath me, roll back to the floor.

ROMANCE OF THE OLD

I am untrue. As untrue as in the old days, the to-be-responded-to letters a pileup in an ivory bowl. How coyly I kept up correspondence! A letter written with "my usual" charm, though mostly exhibiting a muzzled, reined-in quality. *Ex. 1*: to a friend, some tidbits about my writing and about my mother, about a trip taken with T., much neutrality, viz., "We had a nice time. I love Maine." *Ex. 2*: That Awful Person, a sick yellow feeling, like a gloss, as if someone vomited on the page and then wiped it away, a parceling out and serious parsing, knowing that he whom I met and flirted with in a tolerating sort of way, the equivalent of what you might engage in on a train in another country, quite unfortunately lived very near me; *Ex. 3*: my cousin, the actual and the theoretical embodied: we are close, yes? for we are family, but our connection is made of straw; *Ex. 4*: an editor—*an editor!*—to whom I will remain stiff as a lamp and less illuminating, the note drafted into deep lifelessness, and yet somehow, surely, hopefully, alluring, so alluring that he understands that I understand that he understands that I understand that we are one, essentially; *Ex. 5*:—they continue, the parcelings—though there were exceptions, a few ugly exceptions of action and passion, judgment and persuasion. True is hard to come by. When if ever did I write, in all those years, in my primate language of fear? These letters, they are just aspects, faulty reflections. I would like to start afresh, to tell you who I am. I would like you to write me or just tell me. I'm really listening this time. *Who are you?* I love you again.

A CASE OF MOTHERHOOD

I had a child, and then more children. A child, head turned and chin lifted, eyes shut in concentration, finding in sleep bounties of peaches and pork chops and Raisinets. A child, baby hawk tucked close to my body, flawless rider. A child, amid dinosaurs and their social graces, murmuring instructions, eyes on her creation. A child, decked out in all manner of scarf. A child, smartly outfitted for Washington, D.C., with a stuffed dog in her purse. A child, walking to school, balancing guitar, lunch box, backpack, running clothes, art project. A child, adjusting the mirror in the car. A child, a child—and so many children. She is in her room creating. She is in her room dreaming. She is in her room suffering. The walls of her room have dissolved to nothing.

THE TRANSIT OF VENUS

We lived in New York then. We both wore Paul Smith shirts—you'd found a sample sale where we bought them cheap. I was in the habit of wearing clothes that were too large. My Paul Smith shirt was puffy, yes, but made of fine cotton, a pattern of newspapers (*Le Monde, La Repubblica, The Telegraph*) on a pale blue background. The news: nothing lasts forever, but that wasn't what we were talking about. We were eating dinner in our apartment on Central Park West and 110th Street, and you told me that a new acquaintance— one of the new fast friends you made almost on a daily basis—was a hand photographer and that he offered to talk to me about hand modeling: the prospect thereof, a career of a kind.

A week later we were sitting in a coffee shop on Sixth Avenue. The windows were bright and out there in the city people went where they were going. Our table was oak, glossed and sticky with spilled Cokes and the swab of a gray cloth. We didn't often go out to lunch, being broke, with no perceived margin. We were out that afternoon anyway, waiting for the hand photographer. You saw potential everywhere, like an explosion. You spent the day making up stories, by evening believing them. Some things really did come true: we lived in a doorman building, after all.

The photographer arrived. You carried the conversation. As we ate soup and drank coffee, my hands grew to monstrous proportion, naked, nasty, beautiful hands. I picked up my cup, fingers wrapped around the ceramic with creaturely determination. I held my spoon with all manner of delicacy. I let my hands drop to my lap, unseen and impotent, and then I slowly lifted them back up again, positioning my right hand in a jaunty splay between you and me, my left in a submissive curl by the fork. All the while the photographer listened to you, and sometimes spoke himself about various recent assignments, and later about a kind of wood you both liked in furniture. He did not, to my knowledge, even glance at my hands. He had an overly large jaw and a thin long face overall. He was about thirty, with sparse blondish hair, decked out in dorky, non–New York hiking gear.

At the end of lunch, we spoke briefly about my hands. If I were to pursue hand modeling, I would have to target the "wife and mother" market, he said. I would have to nonetheless and in advance for at least a couple of months, keep my hands in gloves all day and night. My veins were a problem, the road-ways and paths of pale green patterning my skin. A "model hand" had no veins.

I'm attached to my hands. A joke, obviously.

We walked to the subway together, you and me. We'd been going out since college—living together for three years. Where was I going; where were you going? Time away from one an-other in that city could stretch for hours, would easily take up half or more of each day. It didn't seem like our choice, really, rather that we both had busy lives, with jobs and friends and possibilities. What exactly is possibility?

I got a seat on the uptown 1. I pulled my hands out from my pockets and placed them on my knees. We had a dog, two cats, and we'd painted our bedroom Bianchi green, like the bicycle. It was an exceptionally cold winter, but our apartment was hot, especially the bathroom. We had the best bathtub. We ate meals at a small table in the living room near the one window with a park view. I remember lying in the bed together at night, with the red curtains and the pale-green walls, and your pink face.

You didn't always feel the lift of endless, almost fake pos-sibility. Sometimes you were tamped down. We were both op-timists by nature with a propensity for the wry comment. My hand reached out for your head, felt your hair, trailed down further, to your shoulder. Did you know that when humans are touching there is a $1/250$ of an inch separating them, always? It is in that space that great engines of steam and breath and life collide.

CRUELTY

Cruelty was rampant at my elementary school, and I was the ringleader. Even today I live in a haze of false identity.

Walking from the car to the school entrance, I was a subtle threat in my camel hair coat, high-waters, winsome shoes, and socks of different colors. The giant headmistress in her giant handmade skirt stood by the door, like Mother Gigogne of *The Nutcracker*. I smiled in complicity, then looked away. Off to the cubbies to hang up my coat and put away my hat, smooth the static from my hair.

During reading hour, Christina and I pored over my secret booklet filled with spells and incantations (my mother had bought it for me at the grocery store). Our teacher saw us, saw the book, wrested it from me. Mother Gigogne was brought in; parents were called. My shame felt physical. I had been holding the little booklet with the pink cover under my poncho. We had not meant any harm. We were powerless. We had no power.

Witchcraft thwarted, I went back to everyday methods, and this is where you'll find me now. I've made Charlene (Mother Gigogne's daughter) into the embodiment of embarrassment, a junior nun, a pat of butter. Heather is a deer in a stand of trees, the way she hides in her parka. Jonathan, first crush— I've rendered his parents into ideas, his father a "father" and also a "rabbi" and his mother just a "mother."

I IMAGINE TIMELESSNESS

Everything is all right at my father's. We arrive just after noon, and Dad and C. emerge from the living room to greet us in the kitchen. "The match just ended, perfect timing." We all hug, six hugs in all. It has been a year since we last saw them. It's always like that: a year, more than a year, almost a year. Apportion life like this and here's how many units you get: fifty to one hundred. If a tree had that many leaves it would be a sparse tree. If a glass had that many drops of water, it would be a small glass of water.

For lunch they've made sorrel soup with vegetables and herbs from the garden, and we'll have cups of that along with ham-and-cheese sandwiches with heirloom tomatoes and lettuce, also from the garden. My father prepares each sandwich carefully, a short-order cook in a country kitchen. C. has made iced tea with mint in a white tin pitcher with red trim, and we pour it along with lemonade into red cups: Arnold Palmers. Our daughter has one, too—venturing. We eat on the porch. A huge sugar maple shades the front lawn. Across the road is a field. Nothing in view but trees, fields, bushes, flowering plants, and our rental car in the driveway. The nearest town is ten minutes away and it has four businesses: a convenience store/gas station, a restaurant, a pizzeria, and a hardware store.

Being here is almost exactly the way it is in my imagination, and almost exactly the way it was during my last visit. Stacks of books on tables, wildflowers in vases, so much bounty from the garden and from local farmers. Dad and C. drink rosé in the summer. Their favorite is from the region of France where they went a few years ago, a vacation made possible by the frequent flyer miles C. accrued when she worked at the magazine. During this week's stay, we'll drink rosé with:

Grilled strip steak, corn, yellow bean salad
Mexican pork casserole, cole slaw, green salad
Pasta with fresh pesto, green salad
Grilled striped bass, caprese salad, yellow-and-green-bean salad
Baby back spare ribs, corn, potato salad

Every dessert includes fresh fruit and Snow's vanilla ice cream, made at a creamery nearby.

For three months, C. has been taking a new drug in an experimental trial. It has been working well, so we've heard.

On this trip she's wearing long sleeves and leggings though it is August. This detail eludes me at first.

It's timeless here, yes—though there are small shifts, of course: a metal clip on the kitchen trashcan's lid to use instead of the foot pedal, a coffee table moved from the converted chicken shack (my father's office) to the living room, two new cats rather than old Emma. Still, the overwhelming sense is of coming home. C.'s address book, taped together and stuffed with papers, by the phone in the kitchen; the collection of earthenware pitchers, the landscape paintings, my father's gardens. I stand looking out the window in the kitchen. I walk around the back lawn. The air itself is familiar, the beauty of the place settles comfortably upon me, I like it here.

The at-homeness is in my father's face, shadowed under a dirty old University of Arizona baseball cap, and in all the rooms, and in the food and in the wine, and it expands out to the places we walk, my husband and daughter and I, and the tour my father gives me of his gardens, and the roll of the roads through the hills on our way to town or from the airport or back to the airport. I've never lived in this house, but I grew up in this kind of country, and so I settle into the rightness of grass and underbrush and trees that have grown for hundreds of years.

We watch the Olympics. We play Scrabble. My daughter wins, thanks to an X in both "ox" and "ax" and a Z in "zero." We play again, as teams. One afternoon Dad drives us to the lake and he sits in a folding chair and reads the newspaper while my daughter and I swim for an hour. She conquers her fear of the tall diving board and dives in, again and again. We eat pizza and blackberry ice cream afterward. At the hardware store, the proprietors always talk to us, like long-lost friends. We are known because of my father. He talks of us when we are gone. We are legends here.

I like being a daughter.

I like asking my father for a dollar to buy an ice cream cone at the hardware store.

I like listening to a conversation between my father and my daughter.

In the dark I lie awake because we have heard different stories now about C.'s condition; a friend told my husband things are worse than she's let on. I've tried to put my stuff away here, tried to help with the dishes. It's hard to know how to help because she is such a gracious hostess and a chef extraordinaire.

This universe is stable, I tell myself, an incantation. This timelessness, this sweetness, these vases on these shelves and these wildflowers.

PANCAKE FLOWERS

I am nervous. I feel completely nervous now, and usually I'm at least pretty nervous. Sometimes I hit a plateau of calm (but usually I'm nervous). If the circumstance is promising, say I'm meeting someone for coffee, or I'm about to talk in an official capacity, well, I'm a bit jittery going in, then there's a sliding descent, and, ultimately, the moment when I become a large person smashing a flower into a pancake, or a large person trying to pick up a tiny flower and put it in a tiny vase on a tiny dresser. Granted, afterward I may experience a kind of calm, or ennui, or at least the mild contemplation of what could have gone better. Usually nervousness comes in anticipation and planning of what I'll do, rather than what will be done to me, but there are exceptions. If there is a flying around of something, a buzzing, darting motion with possibilities of quick nesting and attachment, this gives me a completely different kind of nervous feeling. Let me add that there is also a jumpy intoxication that occurs if I'm standing close to the tracks on a subway platform and a train barrels in. But nervousness itself is not a train; it's more of a boat, a canoe with a solid seat and a long oar I've got both hands on. A person might ask, and with good cause, does gravity keep us up, or is it solely there to keep us down? We remain footed on the ground, but we're not smashed to the ground. Leaden air does not smash us down like pancake flowers, except for when we sleep and dream.

HEART

The heart technician has a shelf full of mysteries to read when she isn't reading hearts. I close my eyes and try to go to the beach in my head, perhaps have a Guinness, while she is reading my heart. Thank you very much, I would rather abstain, for I've already taken the measure of my heart. Here is a small and important valve that moves like coral or leaves in the wind. Not everyone's heart beats in time. Turns out a secret tribe of oyster robots runs this place. How does it start, life? *Pa-thunk?* I'm terrified. I'm in love—with my heart. This is the sound of what can be carved out from underneath my skin. A fingertip, an orchid. I think the heart technician must have been drinking last night. She dyes her hair black. She is of a certain age, when hearts start to give out. I am a suitcase that contains a heart. *Ka-thop, ka-thop, ka—a—thop*. Hearts are commonplace. My husband and I have laid our hearts on top of each other and stitched. No political affiliation, can't dress it up. Even naked, you are a sheath for the heart. The heart technician is relentless with her little knob—she's a bitch who doesn't even notice the sheath part. The sound my heart makes is the sound my daughter heard when she was inside my body. She had her own tiny little heart back then, and now it's grown to be a medium heart. My heart is bothering me. Bland brown cereal is good for the heart. Once upon a time my heart, my dreams, and I were cavemen. The strands of my heart reach all the way up to my throat, and all the way down to that whole other soft part. She's taking my heart by force. I'm about to have a heart attack. She's a tin man. She has no heart. My heart is slurping. It's a sea anemone. It's a seahorse. This throb is killing me. If this ever ends and I survive, I want to smash my heart back up near my husband's heart. I want to use my heart to do some Christmas shopping and cast an absentee ballot. I'm a rickety sculpture where my heart lives, I'm a tree, I'm a birdhouse.

LAKE CHARLES, LOUISIANA

My grandmother lived and died here. I've been here before: I've seen the picture of the girl squatting on the beach, crabbing. Another photo of people on a boat, cat's-eye glasses and cardigans. Now I'm back, more than forty years later. Suicide: something that lasts forever.

Crawfish étouffé, jambalaya, bread pudding. I stare out the hotel window at a parking lot and a billboard, willing ghosts, listening to baseboards. The drive-in daiquiri shack was probably here. The pharmacy was probably here. The whistling air—it was here.

Vivacious, vivid, *Vogue*. They say for years afterward her

husband dressed and cared for her, dolling her up as she slept. Coma: a place you have been before. Where does loss begin? In the center of the subject, and then it moves on, infecting others.

On the way to the airport we park in front of the well-kept, pale house. You could lead a good, vaguely cosmopolitan life here. I squint at trees—probably new ones, since then. The street is a dead end. After hurricanes they build new houses on old foundations in Louisiana.

THE MAUVE NOTEBOOK

When I was a child, I had a small square notebook with French words and an etching on the cover. It was a color I don't love, mauve, the etching in dark-red ink. Inside, I collected quotations. *Shoot for the moon. Even if you miss, you'll land among the stars.*

I used austere, forward-slanting, adult handwriting. My plan was to fill the pages with sayings, gathering to myself the words that would hold me together. I scanned books and magazines and waiting room walls. Kittens in peril, squirrels snacking. You could find plenty of advice at the dentist's, or in school offices, or just about anywhere. *We are all in the gutter,* I added, going with the celestial theme, *but some of us are looking at the stars.*

The yoga instructor asks us to do a pigeon pose toward the end of the hour. It's a lean-over-your-bent-leg situation. I get the feeling/thought of someone. Someone is trying to spread my legs, and I'm trying to close them. It's a picture stored in my hip socket. There's a triangle between my knees and the middle of me, *must keep closed, must keep closed*.

Opening.

The shoot-for-the-moon quote isn't actually in the mauve note-book, I discover, finding the notebook in a banker's box in my storage room. Nor is Oscar Wilde. Nor did I start it when I was a child.

I wrote in the mauve notebook my junior year in college, after the summer I spent in Newport, drinking what was left of my mother's liquor cabinet (Rebel Yell was my favorite, for the trashiness aspect). I'd worked all of June and July as a locker girl at the International Tennis Hall of Fame, read-ing *Tropic of Cancer* on rainy afternoons, or when waiting for tennis players to need new towels or toss me old ones. In the sober, narrow writing I remembered, rather than the moon quote, comes this: *And maybe, when they were left alone with them-selves, when they talked out loud in the privacy of their boudoirs, maybe some strange things fell out of their mouths too; because in that world, just as in every world, the greater part of what happens is just muck and filth, sordid as any garbage can, only they are lucky enough to be able to put covers over the can.* Then Goethe, Cocteau, and a Yannis Ritsos poem.

At the same time I'm thinking about the moon quote and the mauve notebook, I'm thinking about a party I went to in high school. At this party they called me Brandy. I thought it was fun to have a nickname. A girl who likes to drink brandy. A driveway. Men. The gutter, the stars, the moon, *sordid as any garbage can.*

Where, then, do these other images come from? Memories, we'll call them—though they don't just verify but also, being mutually exclusive, fuck up my original recollection:

—Me in my bedroom at 10 Sunset Hill, where we lived until I was eleven, lying on my bed and looking out the window to the driveway, thinking about the moon quote.

—Me on my eighth-grade trip to Washington, D.C., discovering the moon quote etched in marble at the Lincoln Memorial—I'm looking up at the ceiling, which is difficult in my brace, so I'm more like a hardcover book tilting.

At the party where I was called Brandy it is certain or at least likely that some pushing went on. Legs opening, legs closing. Sitting on a man's lap (fun!). A sense there was more than one fun man at the party, paying attention to me.

Laurie, or another girl, might have first come up with the nickname Brandy.

The notebook's cover illustration is of three animals, *le renard, le loup,* and *le cheval,* invoking, according to some unverifiable sources I've just consulted online, a folktale by Jean de La Fontaine. But I probably never did check the origins of *le renard, le loup,* and *le cheval* back when I was in college, and so associations with the fable, which I've downloaded into a PDF, are of glancing value, or irrelevant.

The mauve notebook contains a sequence of stills. It contains ratios of intent and rebuff, of violence and culpability. I can't remember when I was raped because it felt like I was getting raped all the time. I know this wasn't the case, logically.

> *because these and those both were hunted*
> *because of this, only because of this, I told you lies*

Anyway, I was a child.

The trick is to remember the truth, or to experience a sense of truth when remembering. I am lying faceup in the stars, a hammock of threads from one to the other, a constellation. Or I am lying faceup, the stars above me.

HEADGEAR

I open my eyes, which is, to begin with, a deep abrogation, denial, and slight of the black screen within. In there (you know where I mean, we've met there, naked and frank for a change) is a whole other set of recollections, premonitions, and alterations I can't even get into right now. Keep in mind that what I'm saying from here on in, about the so-called life I'm leading? True, yes, important, sure, but unequivocally, cue the blackness, *not the whole story*. So, anyway, eyes open—*oh, to be pitched once more and quite completely out of my cocoon, out from under my velvet snake man, my black jaguar*—my initial perception is one of full-on and obedient immersion in the space-time continuum, nary a time machine in the air. No planes of image, no gnats of recall. Everything around me is pure surface. An ivory dresser. A window with a grate. Textured, rough plaster. A white door. A gold glass candleholder. Cold to the dream, I sit up. I go to the bathroom, come back to the room with the ivory dresser. On a small white table in the closet is where I store my hat. Thank you, Africa. Thank you, church ladies of all sorts. Thank you, Easter. Thank you, Kentucky. Thank you, satanic Arizona sun. Thank you, sports teams. Thank you, civilized men from other eras. Thank you, rappers. I pick up the hat. Thank you, Queen Elizabeth. Thank you, Carmen Miranda. I put it on, and I go, I go like a hustling marathon runner, I go like in a slow motion immersion docudrama. I have wandered the ritualistic netherworld, and now in my tentacled hat I will make a break for it, lowering my head and leaning into the gleam.

DEGRADATION

From the beginning but especially in the city years, I have sacrificed myself for my art. We were all doing it, or so I thought. The fact is, some of the embarrassments tilted to shameful, and I hesitate to tell you about them—about their sheer existence, and then about the systems. It was the systematic part that was frightening. I remember one night, the dark tan of the man with implied cash. His phone number had too many zeroes and a 7; it was the kind of phone number used by corporations. We all marched to the building and then went up the elevator in shifts. I was in Group 4. When we got to the top floor the door opened and I could see the degradations going on in various stages. Someone pushed me from behind—a woman in dark blue silk, one breast exposed. They divided us and divided us. Soon I was in a group on the far left, and it was time for the inspection. We had to open our mouths and they looked in with a flashlight. We had to pull down our pants and show ourselves. Does that wording imply that what is in my pants is all of myself? It felt like all of myself then. I didn't at all like the man who was doing the inspecting, he or his stupid partner. He was a fastidious student-type with glasses, and she was spectral thin with dark hair, bright lipstick, and again with the glasses (though hers were huge round ones). She was in charge of the paperwork. How much exactly did I want to write? A story, two stories? A novella? There was a formula that had to do with page length, but also with content. You had to hand it to them: they knew how to spook you. How did they know I intended to write about my family, about my departed lover, about the nameless dread and the shenanigans? We finally decided I would write one story with allusions to family but mostly following what would seem like a through line in and out of my most recent love affair (not just an affair—a building!), with unlimited access to the dread quotient. That was the most personal part of the degradation. Next came payment. I could pay in various ways, bug-glasses-with-bitter-edges told me, her thin hands cupping triplicate copies of the contract. I chose blowjob to corporate executive. "Same guy as before?" she asked with malice. The ritual was as you'd expect, the klieg lights and the interjections from those who watched and recorded. Audiences had gotten less polite over time, and when I rolled my eyes to the side, getting a glimpse, they weren't even in their chairs: they were roiling in a mass. I was kneeling, using even my abdomen muscles, that's how energetic this situation had become, and my audience had transformed into a peasant wedding, with steins, and grabbing, and stumbling of their own. How would they accurately rate me? The ratings mattered—there was a star system, and I could get an extra poem if I rose above a 4.9 this time. *Pay attention*, I wanted to yell. *Look at what is happening.*

THE HEADMISTRESS

In our town, we try to hold onto what we have during the time we have it. We are eating dinner with our family and we say to ourselves, *I am eating dinner with my family. I've never been happier.* We go for walks and we try to see everything and smell everything, and we gently urge vitamins upon our spouses. When our children grow up, we say, *This is natural*, as if that is a consolation. The headmistress stares at us, she with her sheathed and milky tongue, a glimmer in her eye. She too once had a family. Now she only has a tattoo with their initials on her muscled arm, and in calligraphy above her breasts: *Forever Alone*. We know she is sterner than most, sterner than she needs to be to fulfill our expectations. Despite it all, she continues to surprise us, which we are sorry for.

BIRTHDAY

On my fortieth birthday I swam in the Liffey, or my tears were mixing with the Liffey, or I was pouring a beer into the Liffey, or I took a photograph of a man pissing into the Liffey.

It was a good birthday. My red pants had yet to be stolen. Our computer had literally flamed out, so we couldn't check email too often. In fact, all our communication devices had been disabled.

The entire city was celebrating. I purchased lemon soap. Singing people? Storytelling barflies? It's hard to breathe on one's birthday, especially a round-number-type birthday. *Click, click, click*—you're dead. A series of maps had been drawn up.

We studied them. We intersected often with the stories the maps told, though some of them were contradictory, and all were old and had a chunk of lies within. Once we found ourselves in front of a large gray building. Another time we imagined, but never went into, a bar where the journalists went, and the writers, when those were the same person.

In my dream I told parables to deaf people who were consulting runes. It was like looking down at a map of a city. Everything was shifting and staying still also. I think I am a city person. All these streets go west. The wind is at our backs. I will cross over the river two times.

THERE ARE SOLUTIONS, I HAD
TOLD MYSELF, TO CHRISTMAS

It is Christmas. I go home. I have my new steno notebook. The door opens—behold, the soft umbilical folds, the gastrointestinal maelstrom.

It was going to be an experiment.

Everyone is here. They have taken time off from my dream world to become who they are, in this unnatural naturalness, "reality" they're calling it. I gravitate toward the bowl of nuts. I am talking, too, so as not to raise suspicion. "The train was pretty empty; I was surprised. Maybe everyone is already where they were going." I'm chomping on an almond and my words are falling flat, silencing the room.

Turns out we all agree the weather is dandy and it would be a novelty to go out on the porch with mimosas in chilly hand and stare at the browning. My father says, " . . . ," and I say, "Oh, Dad," and I touch him on the small of the back, in part affection, in part reprimand, in part trying to get to the one last chair that is unoccupied.

I consider my strategy. Time to implement? The actual or potential players in the drama: Father, Mother, Sister, Brother, Sister's Husband, Brother's Wife, Mother's Sister.

My mimosa has vanished. *Damnit!* I'll have to pace myself, I think, so thirsty. The conversation is about the new automatic garage door. My sister's husband is at the thirty-percent mark, I estimate, of an oral essay on automatic garage doors. My sister is staring with tragic conviction at a bush. I grip the patio chair, attempting to get ahold of myself, not to let the quicksand take me down so soon. "The lousy Home Depot clerks, you could sue their asses. If a little old lady bought one of these? Was crushed when trying to hobble in and get her watering can?"

"I've got to get some more nuts and another mimosa!" I say, louder than I'd intended, jumping up with runner's might. I smile at my mother on the way in. The holidays wear on her, the way she feels in the center of things, the decorations, the shopping, all the counterinsurgencies and societal expectations—the sweater I purchased for her would not make up for it, not at all.

Alone in the kitchen with the nut supply. And these aren't just any nuts. This is the nut mix we always have, that my parents always buy.

In this story, my mother and father are together.

This father has a barrel chest and a hearty laugh and a black sweater and a gleaming gold watch and skin that is a healthy, mature, not frail color. He is not as funny as my real father, nor as intelligent.

Picking through the bag for walnuts, I think: I will buy some of these nuts when I get home, a little part of home. Inside me I have a small man in a black suit sitting at a baby grand and singing a sentimental song, singing with resonance and flair, a languishing melancholy look in his eye, and a Scotch with melting ice and condensation on the glass and napkin sitting before him also, on a coaster.

Everyone comes in. My father opens another bottle of champagne, refills all around, and we all go sit in the living room. The house smells of lamb roast. Is this a traditional Christmas meal? It is in this world. In the living room, I gaze at the tree. It's the one I grew up with—literally—for it is not real, but made of the best synthetic needles money can buy. The pine infuser is on the mantel, behind an embroidered felt elf, Norwegian style. There's a stocking hung for the black-and-white cat; it used to be for the other black-and-white cat.

I am not writing this story now. I am writing it twenty years ago.

"Have you heard from Daddy?" my aunt asks my mother, which is odd, since their father is dead. Her tone is layered, like a sweet sad pastry. "He called at Thanksgiving," my mother mumbles, bent over the credenza, pulling out platters and strangely shaped spoons we almost never use.

My fingers are coiled elegantly around the champagne

flute. I'm beginning to remember things differently. Our beautiful trees from childhood: we'd go and pick one out in a street lot, from a church or a boy-scout troop. . . .

Now the pretzel-shaped spoons and spoons for lepers and harelips are on the table in the adjoining room, laying in a dental row upon the lace tablecloth. I squint. I believe the lace tablecloth was made by my mother's mother's mother.

This living room is very much like my current neighbor's living room, which has a comfortable couch with floral slipcovers, two Queen Anne chairs, a bench with satin stripes, a mahogany cocktail table. We're a little crammed together. My brother-in-law is looking at his phone. The ghost of my aunt's husband is standing in the corner, as gaunt as he was at the end, thin and tall as the frequent hallucination I used to have in my parents' bedroom, the green apple man.

"We have something to tell you," my father says, putting down his drink and looking at each of us in turn.

"Wait," cries my mother from the kitchen. I hear what sounds like a pan dropping.

My aunt's face is inscrutable as a dried apple. Kyle puts down his phone and flashes a teeth-whitened smile. I take one last glamorous sip from my mimosa, and then I take another one. The man who is my father in this story is restlessly spinning his gold bracelet. (A bracelet? On my father?) Yet he is not an egotistical man, nor a vain man. He is the kind of (powerful) man who can wear jewelry, like little pelts, pelts of golden mice hanging from his keys, his wallet, his wrist, his neck. The little golden mice eyes are hollowed out and yet still staring. The tails are like ferns or pony manes.

My mother comes back and sits down, and my father takes

her hand. I hold my own wrist, awkward as I was in seventh grade.

"We are moving, moving away, this is our last Christmas together here in this house, we love you all, we can no longer play these roles, it is over, you are lucky to have this much warning, usually it happens out of nowhere, there is no last lamb, there is no last bowl of nuts, usually it all disappears in a puff of smoke, behind the curtain."

I am instantly skeptical.

"It has been—" says the mother figure. She stares toward the soft sculpture of the elf with the pine infuser behind it, and I waver in my convictions.

I ENVISION A FUTURE

I'm walking to the cemetery, but I'm not looking for a shortcut, baby, sings my daughter in her bedroom. I'm in the kitchen, and what I first hear is *I am* looking for a shortcut. Is this a mask, something I might have written at her age? Now my husband leans in the doorway to her room and says, *Hey, I like that.* In the hall I ask him to repeat the line. It's not *am* looking, it's *not* looking. Therefore I can admire it, this lyric.

I wake up one gray morning pitched in sadness. The word *premonition* has attached itself to something I cannot locate.

On the highway's exit ramp, a warren of pavement and broken glass, the meth head, a woman of indeterminate age, walks a slow path, holding her sign down by her navel, *I am homeless, god bless*, a large red plastic cross gleaming against her tank top. Her limbs are lean and brown. Her ponytail is a promise that came and went. We do not give her a dollar. We have vacation road buzz, and the light has changed.

My parents live in a netherworld. The infinite preparations are macabre. I cannot sustain this. I cannot accept a last conversation, or look at belongings as clay and cloth. I sit on the edge of the slide and peer down at endless water. Intent lives within me like a stick puppet.

I tell myself that certain sadnesses, let's just say two or three things I really wish had gone otherwise, have redolence, a little something they bring to the table. Life must include sadness, yes? Though it can so easily get out of control, with the suspiciously likely death situation (nothing? hell? suffocating spaces?), and the gamey hams, and my collected still lives of near-rotten fruit. What does it mean if I say, *we don't choose our portion*? I've learned to watch for the terrier on the roadside, that little harasser. On the stool in the kitchen, I close my eyes and squeeze my fists into my face. If I concentrate.

DON DELILLO

I have always liked Don DeLillo. Well, who wouldn't? I mean, of the writers I know? There are some perhaps who think he is cold. I say: you cannot be cold and write. Your fingers become stiff. Some say: he writes frequently of the same thing, it's a shtick. I say to those people: we all write a shtick of a kind. So his is a large shtick. It's a cold large shtick—and your point is? I have one or two friends who say that in person he is really strange—not the type of person you'd like to spend time with. Oh, but come on. Those people probably don't know what they're talking about. They may not have even met the guy. Do you want to take their word for it? Seriously? I don't think he's running for political office. And who among us *isn't* strange? I'm a little more bristly now, too, less likely to up and make friends at a moment's notice. Granted, I don't like the bitter aftershave: it's scary, it's Germanic—and he tucks in his turtlenecks. That is true, I won't deny it. But that shouldn't be a deal breaker. Where does he keep his books? Fireplace mantel? I don't believe that for a second. I just can't see it. How many copies of each? Two makes sense. I'd do two. I only do one, in my modest corner, but I'd do two if I were Don D. and I was keeping the books on the mantel. You want to fill out the whole mantel, for one thing. It's plain silly to say you simply don't like anyone called "Don." Call him Donald. Not better? Don is okay, I think it's okay. It's just a name. I didn't read the article by Franzen. I might have read it, but it was a long time ago. I know Franzen comes across as fawning. You can't hold that against Don DeLillo, though. What would you do if *Harper's* wanted to interview you? I'd talk to the young writer, myself. You can't hold that against someone. Anyway, I've always thought his prose is really strong. It's keen. It's strong. I like that cold thing. That laser look. Brittle, you say. Right, brittle, whatever, yes. But a chandelier is brittle. Peanut brittle is brittle. Brickle? I love Don DeLillo. I don't know how many l's are in his name. He's a rock star. That Moonie wedding thing? Good stuff. A guy watching a video of a girl watching a murder? I'm there with you. He wears tweed with the black turtleneck, and that's classic, it's standard, nothing wrong with that. Seriously, this man is a literary icon. No writer is famous? Not on Huff-Post? Not on Entertainment Tonight? Ninety-five percent of all folks and 100 percent of folks at Walmart wouldn't know him from Adam? I don't go there. Not fully relevant. I live in the world where if you say you don't like Don DeLillo everyone looks at you like, what are you talking about? Look, admit it, he's one of the absolute main old white guys. He's not just an old white guy but he's a po-*mo* white guy. That is the best. He's all—literarily certified. So don't fuck around. If you don't like him, fine. I like him. All the people at this cocktail party like him, this excellent party on a barge on a forgotten channel. We have our Budweiser. We have our pretzels. And we know Don DeLillo is cool. I can't deny it; I can't change it. *I just like Don DeLillo.* Are you with me? Say the first thing that comes to mind.

THE POWER OF SEX

The power of sex cannot be underestimated, said I, sitting in the tub. I tried saying it again, with richer overtones. The power of sex, I said, feeling the words down in my throat, a rumbling like thunder, *cannot be underestimated*, I then squeaked.

I waited.

I stared at the unpleasantly modernist "perspective exercise" of my thighs and my feet way down there, a little sturdier than necessary for this day and age. A profound amount of ticking and humming was going on in the world at large. The small men and women, they had cast their gazes up from their toil with the hybrid cattle and radish crops, and they were standing near their thatched cottages, watching me with wide still faces, taking in the enormity of my thought.

They knew, I knew. They had experienced their own secret heat under tawdry blue blankets. They had been bestowed with prizes at large performing arts centers, and on such nights, broken strands of pearls in public bathrooms. They had seen it in themselves, urges besting the virtues of modesty and decorum. Up against their poor little cars—Tonka trucks and Mattel police cruisers. You can never get the damn doors open, but who cares when you can lean your inch-high self against the inch-high side of the car, lay your miniscule arms above the small roof, making little dents with your teeth.

I sat silently for a long while. What is power, thought I, a sorrowing giant, only longing to give a daisy to my little peers.

KINDNESS

I am frequently kind. I was kind enough to feed the clunky horse a ball of tinfoil; she took it, so blame passes from one entity to the other. I have just turned my back on a stray cat, betrayed by her lank shank, the subterfuge in her approach, her softness. Fifteen minutes prior, I'd imagined my own cat disappearing and then returning—and my weeping, a fine drama. My husband is frequently the recipient of my kindness. I remind him of all the jobs I'm doing. I'm ill, so ill, I mention—as I stand by the dishwasher, emptying. It is helpful and probably comforting for him to know what a can-do worker he has for a living companion. The exclamation points in the email are mini-shovels, heaping kindness. And there was when I complimented the person from whom I wanted a favor— when I asked the favor, and then after, when she denied it.

THE MIDDLE PART

The middle part of my life was one of desiccation. The white buildings had yellowed in the intervening years. They were yellow with tilted fronts and windows of such gleaming possibility. No one had been saved.

You could—and I had tried to—walk along the wet gray road into another time, but you got tired before you were far enough to make any sense of things, to get out. The crumbled walls and the wrecked fences—they almost made a sound when you walked by. I held my hands over my ears. Eventually I felt it in my ribs and shoulder, an ache, as if I'd been pushing against something heavy, flung myself repeatedly in a carnival ride.

Along the horizon was a line of what I thought for a long time were horses, black shadows with not enough to eat. Burned trees, bushes. I never did have a photo album. All the gleaming clearness, page after page. I knew I'd had a family once, loads of lovers, possibly even children. Some limbs I found: I lashed them on with rope and yarn and wire. I walked with a flopping motion. Standing in the wreckage, I stared. When lucidity came, I was cold under my skin. I sat down on concrete. If I kept looking, if I kept and kept and kept looking—

The buildings were in my way. You couldn't see through them.

A SENSE OF SICKNESS

All the artists are sickly. It's a thing. It started, naturally, in the eighteenth century. It was (and is) related to the wearing of black clothing, in particular black cloaks and black velvet jackets. It's not the kind of sickly that results in imminent literal death, but is indicative of a long, nay, interminable, middle passage—crimson lips and bleakly thin hands, holding onto the implement.

We live mainly in New Orleans and Venice. There is a faded, languishing glory, a deadly opulence, to our affects and our surroundings. We had family—*curse it!*—family we had to wrest ourselves from, family with dark violent power and great secrets. A magistrate or two. Lineage, illumination, inarticulacy. We write out words such as that. We are prone to wearing gaudy emerald rings, heirlooms of course, for they weigh down and anchor our trembling hand.

At times we simply keel over, prior to the completion of our life works. That, however, is something I'm attempting to avoid. The question is: life work? One must make use of every moment, trembling in the cool corners of boarding houses and under-furnished studios, giving it a go. One. More. Word. Must. Write. One. More.

Before death comes!

(We are prone to the dramatic.)

But sickliness isn't finally too elaborate. It feels simple, very plain, when it comes right down to the days and hours. The sickliness—it's a kind of enemy, I see now. If I were healthy— why, I could be out there, in the light, speaking to the newspaperman. Pockets filled with chestnuts and pencils from golf tournaments. I would not even think of my spine, curved as a seahorse, as I looked up in stupidity at the sun.

THE RESTAURANT OF AUTHENTIC FAMILY ARGUMENT

We were at a special restaurant, on holiday, and it was unusual for us all to be together. Who was this "all"? Not *all* all, but those that remained. And one that would not stay.

The restaurant specialized in game. Game: animals that are not penned, raised and tended, but are on the loose in fields and in the forest, and in such environs are finally gunned down. Another word for this is sport.

Does it even matter what the argument was about? It could have been about something in the past, or it could have been a hypothetical, abstract argument. I don't remember the argument, which makes me less sure-footed—not as sure-footed as the fleeing elk, deer, and bison (although the bison were probably domesti-slaughtered).

However, I rose to the occasion. I was sitting straight in my chair, a glass of special wine nearby, and I used my especially-excellent-at-that-moment verbal abilities to make points. Family argument is like shooting ducks in a barrel. You know where to shoot, and even if you don't know exactly where to shoot, you kill something.

Arguments can be fun. Everyone is listening, even the person who just joined the family and will soon be gone again. Put in your point, allow the other to put in his, take it one step further. There's an acceleration factor, like a water slide. If this wasn't entertaining before, it sure is now.

Torches, torchières, torches, candles, much fire, the appearance of fire. The restaurant was festive with light.

We ate our wild animals. This cabernet? I would call it colonial, an aftertaste of stampeding. After the splatter and feast, appetite slowed. By dessert, there was a bitter chill, like the morning after a house burns down. The red and green of the restaurant had paled but for the clinking of silverware.

LANDSCAPE

I found faith in the West. The road I drove down whirled in the most unaccustomed ways. But I began to know the curves, and I leaned into the wheel. If I'd had a cigarette, that would have been great. As it is, I only had jeans, boots, and a hat. Rain would come, stone-gray sky, a listing to the wheat. Sage bushes bounced by the side of the road, fretful as rabbits. I'd never seen hills like these: lunar was one way of putting it. Red roads wound up and over, brick red, darker in weather. It was nobody's life. That night and the night to come, an American beer in a double-wide bar, purely for entertainment purposes. Black cows assembled in calligraphic huddles, telling me something. Telling me to get the fuck out of the wind. A hawk blew up and tilted backward. Under stones and branches, softness huddled and shook. I had written letters to the people who'd made my life, one each, like crossing off valentines. To have no one. To stand on the side of this road and stare up past the close and into the far and past that into the very far, past the storm and into the knife's gleam of white, where the storm would end, as it had come.

THE WOMEN'S GROUP

There is a certain kind of group I do not join. It's the women's group. The moment arises when the women turn to one another and smile and whisper. I can only conjecture that the comments are about movement, speech, or ideas. The women gather without regard for age or talent, although the oldest and most talented one is an icon of sorts. The woman who reels is not included either. The woman who lunges is not included either. The woman who is positively unsexy is not included either. But the group otherwise is fluid and conversant, this and then that woman having her own smile or whisper. I envision (from my corner) a flood of aphorisms and piercing remarks. I stare forward, a very mild smile on my face, my hands clasped behind my back. Soon, the music will begin again. Dear God, let that be the case.

TWO MEN

I had a conversation with two men. There were a great many problems. First of all, man #1 and I were having a convoluted flirtation. His face had a quality I'd seen in other men: a movie-star man and a dream man. The quality was a moving away tendency, a backing up, like a drawn, thick, green-velvet curtain. His eyes looked like two little ladies being abducted by a hunched charlatan, petticoats fluffed up, butts in the air, arms flailing. *Help! Save us.* He had a clean shirt on. One really can't overestimate the power of a clean dark shirt sheathing a chest, shoulders, stomach . . . the tautness of a chariot, a painting. There is a tendency of the hands to tense and release, to rotate at the wrist, in the viewing and the imagining. Practicing, like a dog in sleep, for the bone dig. Well, is it true or not what they say—the instant animal attraction? Felt on both sides when it comes on like that, or could it just be my private wonder garden? There was the fact that he remembered many details of our previous association. *Do tell,* I said. It was the kind of event where you sat around listening to literature for a while, and then took breaks, and then listened to literature again. When it was time to go to the bar a second time, I went to the bar, the thought being he would follow. Yet he did not follow. And so I became a lover spurned, and had to come face-to-face with my apparent onanism. Ah well, whatever—I didn't make a fool of myself, did I? (Brief recap of conversation in my head.) I'll just order a beer, standing here at the bar by myself—shit, it's a free country. So I had my little drink, and I went back in and there he was—having not received my psychic message but smiling in that muted smoky way all the same, sitting, as it turned out, on my coat. (I smiled in a muted smoky way back at him.) The event ended. Cut to us at the bar, one last drink, not only us but with another man. The other man was a well-known writer (well known to us), apparently a friend with my flirtation. For we were all now standing at the bar togeth-er—flirtation, well-known, and me—and flirtation's clothing was shifting on his body. His clothing was not being plucked off with delicate fingers, as I'd once (inscrutably) imagined. His gaze was not coming/retreating. And this beer was not a consecration. No, flirtation's clothing was ripping off because he was transforming into a regular man, someone who didn't really remember or know me or have a cache of stories, by me forgotten. He went from pristine image/albeit moody fellow, to werewolf-style regular man. Yes, his hands were hairier, and tufts were coming out the top of the clean dark shirt. His buttons strained in an ugly cartoonish way, and he was speaking in a language I literally no longer understood—he and the other man. Perhaps this other man was a mentor or professional inspiration of some kind to him, I guessed. I could not even recognize what he was saying, it was like a different person was speaking than the one speaking just moments or an hour ago. Well, I jumped in, like a cat into a catfight. I plunged into the conversation and started saying weird shit about football. I made a fallacious and wanton point or two. I needed to shout to be heard. They were most definitely not listening. They spoke solely to one another, as brothers, comrades, lovers. This was not at all like being Anna Karenina, I thought with disappointment.

WINTER

I used to be all seasons or perhaps no season, but now winter lives within me. How much more real or cold or white is the winter I harbor than actual snow, thin air, the sky's *take this* stakeout—all the sinister season a floozy, profligate and neglectful, prone to the casual casualty, and also something more calculating, a plot, you not winning at cards or anything. The winteriest winter I know now is North Dakota winter, and that's not even my winter; it's my husband's winter: Dairy Queen tilting under a heap of white, cars left running in a smoking black parking lot, houses hot as static. But me, I was a child in my winter, at the ski lodge in Vermont, my parents a bustling concern, getting the lift tickets, buying hot chocolate in the clomping, melting din. We stayed at a white farmhouse on a lonely straight road. Across the street was a long field with a forest behind it and a fence in front of it: field of white, the fence posts glitches, acquiescence. *You can't get it all, there is no master plan, everything has a limit.* Turn back to the house and the bedroom I share with Alex. A country breakfast: bacon, pancakes, orange juice. Did people really live in these mystifying locations, so far from us? I bought a rabbit fur on the way home for a dollar and spent months/years with the fur under my cheek at night, me, the animal lover. Here is the little skin of a little animal that died violently. Here is what I think of winter now: a tall tree in a repeating forest, no underbrush, the snow a theme, shadows cylindrical and so long, just giant— passing over the solid, the logical, laying out over everything with disregard for your petty bullshit, and a light that comes from the turn of the earth, from planets colliding three trillion light years away, from a pebble turning under a collision of storms, the residue of time, death, passing, journey. Deep utter ruthless aloneness. That's the kind of light. And by the tree is a rabbit, brown roll, terrified.

BIG SLUT/LITTLE GOD

Her nose is deer delicate, a little teacup bone. She's wearing many scarves, flats with Velcro buckles and hexagonal toes. She carries the world around in her satchel—the age of brilliance. Her eyebrows are one of her best features. I like how interesting and beautiful her face is all on its own.

Yesterday I looked through my makeup and realized it's very old. Very old makeup is a problematic problem. It becomes like circus makeup, clown face. I tried some of it on, to see how it was working these years. I rubbed the crap out of my eyebrow so you couldn't see the line of brown under the hair, but rather a kind of smudgy-brown cloud. I checked online to figure out again how to put on eye shadow. Every once in a while I do try to amp up the glamour. I make a personal commitment to putting clips in my hair.

She has a cold right now and her nose is red and her skin is paler than usual. I long to give her a Kleenex or a cashmere throw. She knows I know she is his girlfriend but we haven't discussed this fact because the relationship is under wraps. My station in life is that my hair is going gray. Right now the dye has faded and I haven't made another appointment. Should I "go gray"? Yikes. I went to the pharmacy and stared at coloring kits. When the stylist does my hair, the gray is taken care of, but overall my hair is a kind of weirdish color.

If I love her, it's an overlap. I'm in him, loving her. I am me, thinking about how he loves her. *I'm on the top of the world looking down on creation and the only explanation I can find* . . . I guess I had never completely tried this trick before. No one actually invited me to this party; I'm a voyeur. You don't even want to know how many people I'm in love with right now. I'm the biggest slut in the world.

THE OPTIMISTIC WALK

I advise against walking like that. Your optimism is on display, like a worn leather satchel with one wrinkly white shirt inside. It's the natural gait of a very short—e.g., a one-foot-tall—man. It's not reliable. It's not likely to mean anything. Besides, the kind of person who walks like that—what happens when he lies down? His legs keep moving. That's an unpleasant sight, in the hotel room, on sheets whiter than the shirt, with the map of Madagascar in hand. Swivel, swish. *Hold down, lad. Hold down.*

THE DARK UNDERLORD

I am the dark underlord you've been waiting for. Or at least I hope you've been waiting, because I've been in my lair for a dog's age, trying on outfits for the occasion. Obviously, I want to make an impression. An impression of dark arrival, an impressive impression. I want to come into the room, virtually *appear* in the room, with a swish of lethargic cloth and an upright posture. I have debated between capes, Snapchatted a couple of dubious associates, and decided upon the satin with the purple velvet lining and towering, almost gaudy collar. I admit my outfit never feels quite dark enough. One of the dubious associates suggested rubbing it in dirt—fool. Though he may have been on to something.

But I, the dark underlord, long ago gave up on the appearance of distress. It does not serve my purpose. I understand it can be sexy in a mechanical way, suggesting long, weary struggle, individualism, a totemic nature. So what! I will always shave before I go out, I will always shine my boots. Old school: what of it? It's a *swoop in*, you understand, a vacuum or an illumination. (Not that I am *not* tired—the campaign has been a long one.)

I have come, and I will coerce you, and perhaps something specifically dreadful will occur, for I do not shy away from dread or incident. You may feel comfortable in that static dream, but that static dream shall be, as the associates say, nevermore. I will pull you toward me, and we will collide there in our dark garments (my dark garments, your jeans and T-shirt), and we will roughly make a kind of bleak dry love, battlefield fucking. And then we will be chained together forever (metaphorically). You will have submitted to my stark power.

Alas, there is the issue with afterward.

For I never force the subjects to come with me, actually. I have been in the habit now for several centuries, when no one is looking, after the Sturm und Drang, the television moment, the swoop in and takeover, of releasing the subject, loosening my arm from around the neck of the waif or the fevered husband. It is just us, then. Behind the very large, the overlarge boulder, back in the shadows, the forest of backstage, she or he gets up from her/his knees. Wobbles. Looks at me. I look back, not penitent—not exactly. But it is the moment of truth, I am deeply afraid to say. *Do you want to play in my lair with me, we can try on capes and live on venison, perhaps, and pear spritzers?* It all comes down to now, the boot polishing and the telepathy practice and the infectious laughter. She, or he, has a fragile look at this stage in the game, and yet still—still, to a one—has had the strength to walk away.

THE BAG

I am a bit concerned about the bag. The bag, I feel, does not have enough room in it. Am I claustrophobic? Yes, but it's not my bag, and in any case I won't be *in* the bag. Books will be in the bag, notebooks will be in the bag, binders will be in the bag. Or, I should say: one book, one notebook, and one binder—considering how small the bag is!

Last night I dreamed my husband had died. Or would die. He was alive, but we were reading his obituary. This house is too small for both of us, a person might shout, but actually, this house is too big for just one of us. In my waking life, I'm uneasy about plans for after one's death. Does it really matter at all, or does everything just explode? *Ka-boom!* And it's defunct, all the strange furtive necessity. One must, at least, be mindful of whoever might be in charge of the files and boxes and bags, afterward. One can only hope it *is* boxes, not merely one's little bag, that need attending, though I imagine it will be the boxes and bags and everything else, down to the wallet, down to the nail polish. No, that bag is *not* big enough, I was thinking in an obsessive way when I woke from the dream, one bird chirping, the day about to break.

We could lay things out here on the table, organized alphabetically. Or by size or by place of origin.

Memory—who needs it? My family doesn't, quite obviously, but still it seemed worthwhile to ask my mother to record what she remembers now, when she's at, say, seventy-three percent. In a gesture of compliance, a *Spy vs. Spy* maneuver, I too wrote down some "milestones," as she called them. When I come across this document on my computer later, it looks like a racetrack or a zebra skin. I also find a story without attribution. I read it suspiciously. This is not my font, these are not my metaphors, and overall this stupid fucking story holds no promise. The problem with milestones is that they hang heavily from one's neck—grindstones, drowning stones—despite their occasional accuracy.

If, I say with something masquerading as patience, you need items A and B for school, wouldn't it be great if those items slid smoothly into the bag, instead of needing to be stuffed in or carried separately?

I myself have two purses, my biggish purse, into which I can put a paperback and a water bottle, in addition to my wallet, sunglasses, eyeglasses, reading glasses, small notebook, pen, lipstick, keys—and my travel purse, into which I cannot put a water bottle or paperback, though yes to lipstick and keys. When I am in Tucson, where I keep heaps of paper and some canisters and mugs and plaques with sayings that people have given to me, I use my big bag. When my daughter goes off to high school tomorrow, I'll have plenty of time for myself. Work on the golf game, maybe? In time, my filing will be done. Next: all my pets will die.

QUERY

Where do the drunk people go?
  I go to a place of splendid isolation.

DARKNESS

He wore a gray suit, kept clean and pressed and without stains for many years. The pockets of his jacket had nothing in them, except the inside pocket, near his heart. The kind of pocket I didn't even know existed until much later when I had my own men to consider, wardrobes to weigh in on. He wore a hat outdoors. He had two kinds of shoes: regular shoes, polished black leather with tentacle shoelaces tight and secure, and tennis sneakers, Pumas. I should say, too, he had golf shoes. Yes, I was wrong, he had three kinds of shoes after all.

He lived for years in downtown Chicago, but then he moved to a country club. This was around the time I learned the term *bachelor pad*. A small kitchen greeted you when you opened the front door. There was a living/dining room, a bathroom, and a bedroom with two beds and a cot near the window (for me). I looked out from there, to the city at night, past the horse stable, the tennis courts. To get to the apartment, you had to take an elevator. Near the elevator was a table and on the table were mints on a silver platter.

It sifted down later, like ash. But back then I was brave before his dour demeanor. On rare occasions he'd emit a low chuckle, but most of all he was serious, a serious old person in a suit, his chest caved in like a question mark, his knees jutting as he sunk into the couch, smoking a Camel, an after-dinner indulgence. He brought me on a shopping trip every Christmas. He once said he would buy me a horse. He was a curiosity and a resource, an immutable gray figure, eyes watery as a day that has escaped or will never come.

Maybe I did hear conversations back then, but I do not remember them. He thought the numbers were inflated. What's the difference between this number and that number? Later I began to feel it was quite a lot.

My mother: *He put us before everyone else; he devoted himself to us. He taught us tennis and golf and he never remarried until we were married. All the German Americans had a tough time back then. Boys threw rocks at him.*

What can you know? I look for circumstantial evidence. Does it matter that his country club was a bastion of "tradition," or racism—that membership began to decline as the South Shore neighborhood became integrated, that the club never did allow black or Jewish members?

That doesn't damn everybody in the club, but it's not a good sign either.

My father remembers his former father-in-law as a lonely figure, and he agrees with my mother on this: the man devoted himself to his two girls when they were young.

I see my grandfather in black-and-white, that's what this is, this pummeling rain, it's the black-and-white of photographs, the black-and-white of memory, the black-and-white of *was he a good man?* One must put one's grandfather on the stand, one must ask of one's grandfather: is it true, how could you think that, even if you did get rocks thrown at you?

My father says, *Remember his canaries? He let them fly free in his apartment—this was back on West Harrison Street. The bathtub was speckled with bird shit.* He shakes his head.

Canaries? I didn't know my grandfather had canaries. Into the black-and-white, the relentless gray of recollection, bright flitting yellow comes.

APOTHEOSIS

When I left, my father gave me the May issue of a magazine—one of her subscriptions. He said maybe I'd want it for the plane. On the tarmac I turned the glossy pages, each new image an assault on my eyes. I was thinking of what should have been: *her* eyes seeing these ads, these photographs, liking this boxy purse and this color scheme. I would never forget my father standing on the porch as my brother and I walked away from the house to the car. It was not morning, it was never going to be morning again. Then it was morning again.

We had eaten mightily, stuffing our bodies with ham, macaroni and cheese, pies. We'd sat in the living room surrounded by flowers. Purple, yellow, pink: these are the colors of death. She is everywhere in this room, in this house. She is everywhere in this town, in this country (and in some foreign countries as well). Living, she was confined to her own body, and this was reassuring to the point of invisibility. I could always call her, I could always write her an email, and besides, I would see her again next summer.

DO-IT-YOURSELF
EXTERMINATION

First time I saw the black widow I was impressed. The black sleekness, some polish. She was resting in her web. I shined the flashlight. I had my Raid and sandal. Sprayed her with Raid because I couldn't smack in the space behind the box. When she started to move to open ground I killed her with the sandal. End of story. But there was a next time, and another next time. Webs under the chairs, web by the flowerpot, web by the hose reel. Thereafter came a late-summer vigilance, out nights with my flashlight and Raid and sandal. Peering behind the original box, waiting. In my robe and pajamas, Sleepytime tea cooling inside, a cat ready to jump on my lap, my kid doing homework, we'd all watch TV later. A couple of weeks passed, no spiders. Then one night I saw another black widow behind the box in the mortar of the house. Sprayed the living shit out of her. Didn't bother with the sandal. She curled up in poison. I almost ran into another web—expanding out from a pot on the other side of the patio, expanding everywhere. Spider. Killed it, too. Husband on phone from far away: *They're going to get in the storage room.* I got off the phone and went back to the storage room, turned on the light. A web of webs, a network of webs, four feet from the cat litter box, ten feet from the washing machine. My house. My family. My dog. My cat. Armageddon. I Raided the spider. The next morning I emptied and vacuumed all the closets. Pulled the vacuum cleaner around the house, ramming and yanking. Finally I got myself into the storage room, my goal all morning, narrow corridor, crap everywhere. This time I was wearing gardening gloves and sneakers. Webs illuminated in the sunlight, all over my daughter's old rocking horse. The vacuum worked, but it wasn't strong enough. I pulled the horse out of the way. I moved the blue and yellow and green swim noodles. On top of some boxes was my daughter's old school project: an organic gardening diorama. Glittery crops, four years old, no reason to keep, spider house. Webs between the golf bags. I vacuumed them. I moved to the adjoining room, the laundry room, and vacuumed behind the ironing board and trashcan. Mops fell, an assortment of metal mystery parts fell, the ironing board wouldn't lean the way it was supposed to. I slammed it into the wall (ineffective). Brought rocking horse, badminton set, and milk crate of pool toys outside. Then I left the house.

I drove to Do-It-Yourself Pest & Weed Control. Considered taking selfie for husband in front of store sign, like all killers. Inside the store, a middle-aged, pot-bellied man in a white shirt behind the counter, and a male customer looking at 'cide. I was calm, confident, and determined. The pesticide behind the counter was $24.95.

—Is this safe for pets? I've got a cat and dog.

—They spray cattle and all manner of animals with this. Kills fleas.

—So you're telling me it's safe for livestock?

A "delivery system" was twenty dollars. I could buy one and use the petroleum-based stuff outside and the water-based stuff inside.

—Just wash the tank in between. Customers come in and say they sprayed their roses and the flowers died; it's because they didn't wash out the tank.

He'd been spraying around his own house for a long time, he said. I imagined a fortress, a wasteland, not a single thing living.

—Spray a six-foot perimeter around the house and three feet up the house. That deters them. The airborne insects, if they land, it'll kill them too.

I said something about preventative measures, seal up the cracks, clean up debris? He showed me the direct-kill spray, vanilla-scented. I didn't ask about the lemongrass insecticide I'd seen advertised at the organic place online. I picked up a glue trap.

—Keep your dog away from those, they smell like peanut butter, dog's fur could fall out.

Home again, home again with the direct-spray poison and two glue traps. I placed one trap under a milk crate in the storage room. Sprayed the vanilla poison around the door and the wall. It had been a bad summer, in terms of death. *Die, die, die*—but the battle wasn't over. There had been the time I'd sprayed Raid under the hose reel and a gecko ran out. He headed toward the yard, but he wasn't running straight.

NUDITY

How nude am I? My toenails are crudely cut and I fear not clean enough, either. My legs haven't been shaved in days. My stomach and breasts droop, my thighs are ambiguous. I hurried here—I'd planned to shower and shave before the appointment, but I was sick, so I slept right up until I had to leave. Now under the fluorescent lights, the doctor and intern inspect every inch of my skin. They are, in theory, looking at it differently than I am looking at me. This is actually *not* me, I would like to say. For I usually do shave, or give the appearance of shaving. And I wear toenail polish fairly consistently, in the season. I can't adjust for my age, but otherwise not so bad, eh? I exercise and I don't overeat . . . though I admit I seem rather puffy.

Well, whatever, this is staggeringly humiliating. They're both wearing dresses, and their hair and makeup is in order. I'm wearing a patient's demeanor. But couldn't this demeanor be just a little sharper, cleaner, smaller? Another, very nude me is waving a flag in my brain. *Hello, here I am. I'm having a thought now. I'm making a joke now. But you keep trolling over my body with your caterpillar mouths, with your oven mitts and scalpels. After that come the notes, as you define me.*

FORGETTING

What I do is I write down things I am especially sure I might forget. I am against forgetting. I write dreams down on pieces of paper that slip in with other pieces of paper and are lost. Lost is better than forgotten. I sometimes write down conversations. If someone says something egregious, I write it down before I forget. This is because when someone says something egregious it goes in a certain funnel and is mixed up inside my brain with a volcanic blast of understanding, speculation, and commiseration, and is thus instantly diluted or even distorted. It is then impossible for me to remember what the thing was in the first place. Of course, I am all for understanding, speculation, and commiseration—just not too soon, is what I'm saying. Because of the blast and the concomitant smothering. Is it smart to try to remember words that are confused, damning? I believe it could be, at least, important. But like the dreams, I do not go back to these conversation notes. They are also dreams, shuffled into the paperscape surrounding my desk, leaves fallen off a tree, a dog's stash of bones. When I write things down, these few words develop their own weight and reality, and I can then relax the rest of my brain and not worry so much about forgetting. I am like a little old man leaning on a cane and whistling. The day will surely never come when I gather up these fragments and assemble a model of the life I had. The husks of experience: discard them! And yet, it is a pleasure to tease out the past, which is all of my life. Except for the future, which is, surely, also something that shouldn't be forgotten.

FAULT

Sometimes I get anxious somewhere between being awake and asleep. It is a not-good promontory, a bridge broken. All those splintered boards, spiraling down into emptiness, and then the wrecking waters. Many true disasters are revealed. Top of the list: the reckless ruin that is my own personal responsibility. Now the crows coming to roost, now the hippos in the flower garden, now the splat, the fire, the fingers pointed—as has always been the secret case. Yes, there is black seepage behind the curtain, and he who is (perhaps) reading with ease next to me: he does not know, nor can he save me.

OSCAR WILDE
AND MY BROTHER

When Oscar Wilde and my brother met, the world almost came to an end. I wasn't there, but I heard about it.

This was after the trial and imprisonment. There is no greater challenge to the charming and magnificent than full-on societal ramming. It is difficult, at times thereafter, to feel elation. One is hardly aware of one's fan base, then.

My brother was at the tea shop. Sitting with a cup of tea, reading *USA Today*. He was on a business trip, selling wares, but for an hour or two he'd been freed from meetings. He read the paper and relished his time alone. Infrequent and cherished, a time of order.

He was catching up on sports.

The man he'd had dinner with the night before was a rugby fan.

These people also liked soccer.

And cricket, apparently.

In strolled a man in a velvet jacket. Frock or jacket? It was a faded green garment, like a jacket but down to his knees, double-breasted, worn at the elbows and seams, and also there was a fluffy white shirt. Lace, perhaps. With a defeated, limp look.

My brother wore a yellow polo shirt. He was in his own way a clotheshorse. He kept his polo shirts hung up in his closet, arranged by color.

Oscar Wilde ordered tea. He pulled coins out of his pocket and sorted through them, counting and recounting, and at last put one, then another coin on the counter. The tea purveyor was bored. He swept the coins from the counter and into the till.

My brother watched as the man in pale velvet turned. He flipped his hair from his forehead and strode over to the round café table to the left of my brother's. Exhibiting fatigue or relief, he flung himself down, resting his head against the wall and kicking his butterscotch booties out in front of him. "Son of a British bitch," he muttered.

When my brother looked over, Oscar Wilde's eyes were closed.

The purveyor showed up with the steel pot. He set it and a little basket of necessaries on the table and walked away. Now Oscar Wilde and my brother had identical baskets. Oscar

Wilde set to, pouring the tea, the cream. Ladling spoonfuls of sugar. He was large, like a giraffe or a rhinoceros. He held the dainty cup to his mouth.

My brother was looking at the paper, but he hadn't been following sentences for a few minutes now. Letters were shapes; lines undulated. A play of black-and-white, streaks of blue.

"What?" he said. The man had spoken to him.

"Might you have a bit of cream?" Oscar Wilde gestured toward the pitcher on my brother's table. "Mine's empty."

The man's face wasn't handsome, but it was imposing. Under his eyes the shadows were gray, permanent.

"Sure," said my brother, handing over his half-used cream.

"This place has gone downhill."

"Has it?"

"But then who hasn't? Dogs wear crowns, if you let them."

"Uh-huh."

"Fear not. Capitalism will rise and save the day. All rolls will be buttered and warm."

" . . . "

"The point is I recognize *them* but they don't recognize *me*. What a lark! A positive joy."

"I wouldn't know. I'm just visiting."

Mr. Wilde let out a barking laugh. He rubbed the lace on his chest.

The two men went back to drinking their own tea. With effort, my brother finished the article. He is, in so many ways, a mystery to me.

The tea purveyor was talking loudly on the phone.

Oscar Wilde began to cry.

INTERNATIONAL SUCCESS

In France they got me. Éditions Gallimard, my covers blanched white, titles in red, the font Didot. There were omnibus editions and limited editions and third and fifteenth editions. Walking from the metro, I might see a book on a table or in a lap, jacket torn from fervent readings, white softened to gray. I'd get my own coffee then, and either tuck into a corner, by the waiters' station, or go back to my room and sit on the couch, manuscripts spread out before me. I froze there, a portrait, awaiting something to say.

TIME

For a while there I had a list of, er, lays. Good lord, where did that list go? I hope I didn't leave it anywhere—for just anyone to see. There was, with equal obviousness, my résumé, education and jobs and hobbies and skills. A large pile of journals, chronicling emotional states, mundane occurrences, lays, and here and there a holiday or a persuasive event. There was the slow evolution of product purchase. The winnowing down of Kiehl's, the ramping up of Jergens. The winnowing down of Lancôme, the ramping up of MAC. (Consistent downward mobility?) People did die, though many have also hung on—are clinging here with me, clustered around the doors on Black Friday.

TRAGEDY IS COMING!

When I die, there will be nothing left at all—not a scrap of Christmas paper, nor an olive in the refrigerator. The thought, therefore, is to steadily erode my surroundings between now and then. I have an emery board, and I make use of it. I understand there is a natural accumulation (of dust, of cutlery; the pens and keys in that one drawer) but at the same time there is the terrible fierceness. I can and ought to latch onto this. So: I gnaw, I hack. I toss things off cliffs. I've been patient so far with the animals in my life (some things take care of themselves) and I admit to losing nerve sometimes, with people. But I persevere. For instance with that one friend, we were taking different routes to the store. And instead of going to that store, I went to another store instead. Taught her to think we'd see each other again—it's been six months now, and counting! Electrical or mechanical items oftentimes break on their own, and I leave them in the alley. They disappear, only to show up on a mountain of broken electronics in some far-off ocean-side locale, swarming with beetles and white birds. Have you ever seen a beetle eating a hard drive? It accounts for much, I must say. I'm hoping I break many bowls between now and doomsday. Plates, bowls, cups, glasses. And I keep filing. I file in a hunched over position, eyes fixed and pinky up. Because Britishisms will be one of the last things to go—I'll hold onto my (last) teacup, to my manners when it comes to eating soup or holding open a door for one last old lady before I make her disappear. There are so many personal items. The mattress I have set fire to, the computers, the phones, the jewelry I've sold on eBay. The others, the people, they are still a bit of a problem. Too many to get rid of in any pragmatic physical way, too many to murder. Turn my back? Ignore? Sometimes it strikes me, as I lay in my tent, without my things, except for the towel and the metal cup, and the one flash drive, that this wasn't quite the answer. Admittedly: feng shui, Zen, who likes clutter. But the sun is relentless, the shine of it through the blue fabric. It blooms for so much of the day, and then at night—it is cold here.

THE WRITER

She is laughing uproariously, if only for a moment, before turning away from her interlocutor to find, with any luck, the beer. Perhaps she is not tactful. She is large inside, like a circus balloon animal: puffed up limbs, hips, bust. Her neck is tight with tendons, shoulders thrown back with post-gender rigidity. Of course she cries sometimes and of course she has her own loves and sorrows. The interlocutor is not seeking much, on this particular gay night, but to strike up an intellectual party of two, a little junky glory, just him and her amongst the clamor. Yet at this moment he feels he is wearing a donkey's costume. His head is all furry. Where has she gone? He can only see her tail, a piece of rope with a feather attached, slipping away between the partygoers.

YELLOW BIRD

The yellow bird was dead. My friend had been keeping it in a cage, though she usually left the cage door open. That's what she told me, sitting cross-legged in her living room, tears on her face. "Death is a stern mistress," I said. I had been reading up on it. She was looking at me with what could have been anger. "Death is but an illusion," I then said.

A friend of my friend had told me that my friend had been married five times, not three. In Egypt, back in the day, little boats took you from the place where you were "dead" to a place where you were alive again. If you take away the sense of *individual mosquito*, you will see that they, too, can be reborn.

Oh, I know it's not always easy. Sometimes it's the Lego sky-scraper we're talking about. There's no way we're going back to finish the Hogwarts castle. The huge plastic container of parts remains in the storage room, inert. If we did anything, we'd make something new—a flattened-out eagle, for instance, or a very small paddock. "My little yellow bird," said my friend. I closed my eyes. In a dream I'd gone to her house in the early morning. I needed to wake her up. Instead of knocking on the front door as usual, I walked in the sliding door. The birdcage was inside, by my feet. At first I thought it was empty, but I looked closer and saw, behind the bird mirror, the yellow bird, dusky in the dawn light. When telling a dream to an analyst, you're supposed to use the present tense. In certain kinds of fiction it is effective to make the protagonist trot about in an eternal now. "Did one of your previous husbands give you the bird?" I asked—ever the friend. She looked down and shook her head. I walked through the house in the dream, into the living room, where the shades were drawn, then all the way down the hall to my friend's bedroom. If you think of all the yellow birds that have been plowed under over time, if you think of history, and everywhere, and you think of all yellow birds, whether they are dusky yellow, or yellow with black and gray feathers, or yellow only in certain seasons, mostly very small with delicate bones, but some rather large, majestic yellow hawks with sad eyes and curved beaks, or Big Bird, the largest of the yellow birds that I know of, then, wow, that's a lot of yellow birds to lose. When I think of the yellow bird that I met three times, once in a dream (if it was the same one), once in real life, and once through words in the living room—those other yellow birds become but echoes or lost names, bird chatter as the day brightens, before it gets too warm.

MY GOLFING VACATION

I plan to take a golfing vacation in the lakes region of Northern Italy. I understand the golfing is challenging there. The lakes, and the mountains I have heard, make for daunting rounds. However, I'm not looking toward "retirement"—if that is even the word you'd use—for complete ease. I believe there's a hotel near one of the lakes that specializes in weeklong stays, a few small shops within walking distance—lovely, eclectic places to buy incidentals and food to nourish one for the course(s). I imagine myself strategizing on brief triangles of turf, all my concentration focused on a specific and perhaps realizable goal. I envision brief encounters with new acquaintances, those who speak in another language entirely, or perhaps just speak English with idiosyncratic inflections. I see a small pile of scorecards on a stone-top table, on a patio, underneath an ashtray from another era.

I will not cry too often on my golfing vacation in the lakes region of Northern Italy. That is my hope. I already have a modest stash of golf balls awaiting the day, as well as a white glove.

ICEMAN

I am the iceman, crushed by yesterday. For fuck's sake, I fell flat on my face. Toppled like a wedding cake. This wasn't just a small disruption—a low tire, the insurance company's error— it was a travesty, quite serious. And now, as in forever, my body drapes the boulder like a shroud, a mother's cupped palm. (Meanwhile, back on planet earth. What with the ascent of man and the rise to power and the conquering of civilizations.) All right, let's think about this. Here is how my body lies: with one arm squashed underneath. There was the brief flurry: that soaring free fall from life to death, from what seemed like forever to forever itself, no more twigs and seeds for lunch, not one more even blah installment of the monthly saber-toothed tiger hunt with my reluctant, moody cohort, no more pitiful explosions with my lady friend, her snatch so very contemporary. I heard some kind of trance music—I saw colors of such delicate gradation, such perfect oval symmetry—

And then, okay, forever. I shall be forever. I shall lie here on this boulder, my arm at an (what would be laughably) uncomfortable angle. I shall not close my eyes but hold the grass palace in my retina, the shadow that is Asshole coming to retrieve his arrow. (At least let me keep the arrow. It's so tacky to take the arrow.) And here comes a mountain to lie upon me. Oh, wait: this is a little heavy. The slow shovel of earth, the patient gravedigger, the patient artist, an extravaganza, a sobering bounty. Waves of all you could possibly wish for: the sleek bones of that snatchy lady, the desiccated remains of my enemy's child, the most abundant harvest of fava beans you'd ever want to see, and mountain laurel and lupine and elderberry. Here is a glorious parade of hilarious rabbits, running as if to their own deaths, and here is the tinder of a thousand houses, the rupturing of windows created at great expense, the invention of glass, and here is a telescope with which a pirate found a white-frocked soft spot on a faraway sea, and here is the certificate that stupid state school gave me, saying I could read.

Did the weight of water ever occur to anyone, when they were puzzling this thing out? Did anyone ask *me* if I wanted coffee?

—the mountain with newspapers in it, the bland-faced judges' final decrees, the Polly Pocket dolls, presidents, labor organizers, fat ladies—

—wolves, lesbian deer, lions on the threshold of glory—
The weight did elongate. I become rather long and thin.
The fighty ones with their hot instruments came and said my
stomach was up by my armpit now—well, what of it? Wouldn't
your stomach have moved, too? We get used to having our in-
sides stay in one place, but I'm telling you, it's all a jumble in
there, seriously. You think you're one thing: just a man on a
mountain with a plan for the day—and before you can even
take one more breath you're an explosion of flowers, deep and
bright purples and lacy whites and bruised reds and streaks of
yellow, and when before you could hardly do a box step you are
now Mr. Tall, step-sliding across the night sky.

THE NURSING HOME

Soup to nuts, I reveled in the experience—though at times I thought, *this could end*, and *end* had a nasty resonance, like all the nursing homes could go out of business or something. The fact is you learned a lot, day in, day out, hour by hour. Every minute carried weight and significance, and you had to be careful not to miss it. We're still in the swath of years, understand, when you have to decide to be dapper, sloppy, or go pastel. I'd been working with dapper. Dapper had a lot to do with my triangle pin. As a point of pride, I didn't leave it on the same jacket every day. I jabbed at new fabric every morning.

Then came the powerful moment when ninety-nine percent of all I'd ever owned was stolen, sold, borrowed, or ruined. I still had one frame that dissolved what you saw. My kid, me as a kid, my kid's kid. It was all very entertaining and if I squinted (or just took off my glasses) I could almost hold one image over the next. It was another way to learn something. I still had two coffee cups, the one I used in the morning for coffee, and the one I used in the evening for tea. But if I ate in the cafeteria (they called it the dining room), I simply used the cups they provided.

The social element at the nursing home was always changing. There was a glassed-in case in the living room where they posted, daily, a list of Changes. Sometimes the "Changes" had changed before the change—they'd become vessels of pain. But you couldn't fault the institution on this in terms of categorization. The list was posted above the calendar but you could still see it at an angle from your chair, if you had one.

I liked the helpers. Some were thieves and I've always had a soft spot for thieves. Some were sadists or just stupid people, and I've always had a soft spot for the sadistic or the stupid. Still others were young and caring, and they looked in your eyes earnestly when you were attempting to pee. Still others were priests.

The priests were always up for conversation, even if they did annoy with their positive outlook and their expansive universe ideas.

I didn't remember everything, but who does? I just hoped they were giving me the right medications, and that I wouldn't see Mike again. With the wrong medication came hives or dribbles, at odds with the dapper plan. You could always hope that the fuck up would go in the other direction: dreamland. A friend from a long time ago ended my nursing home experience. I was unprepared for it—unprepared to see her again. The last time I'd seen her she'd been very ill. But then she moved to France. She spent thirty years there raising bees and eating sorrel and being in love. And walking her dog. She came into my nursing home room one day, shortly after my electronic picture frame ran out of batteries and one of the thieves had taken my morning coffee cup, and my pin's pin had fallen off and so I'd had to resort to Scotch tape on my sweaters, and she helped me off the ashamed floral couch where I was watching television. She carried me to the shower, got me all clean, and then put me in some very dapper clothes and we snuck out the back door, past Willy the Moron, and she drove me to the airport, and together we boarded a plane to Paris and when we got there we set up in a little apartment near Gare du Nord, not the best neighborhood but I wasn't complaining, and we set about having picnics in bed and listening to old Edith Piaf and Duke Ellington records until we both nodded off at last, completely dead.

ACKNOWLEDGMENTS

Some of the stories in this book were previously published in the following journals:

"The Transit of Venus," "Sex Worker," "Headgear," "A Case of Motherhood," "Pancake Flowers," "Heart," "The Mauve Notebook," "The Power of Sex," "The Optimistic Walk," "Nudity," *Conjunctions* 69 (2017).

"Cruelty," "Ennui," "Iceman," "Romance of the Old," "Sara Applewood," "Sea Travel," "Silence," "The Dark Underlord," "Yellow Bird," *Conjunctions* 65 (2015).

"I Envision a Future," "The Headmistress," *Denver Quarterly* 51.3 (2017).

"The Middle Part," *Five Points* 17.3 (2016).

"Wolf in the Basement," *Mississippi Review* 41.3 (2014).

"Lake Charles, Louisiana," *McNeese Review* 54 (2017).

Thank you to the editors and readers who have helped me along the way, especially Bradford Morrow and Ander Monson, and my agent, Ellen Levine. Thanks for letting me jump in the pool with you, FC2 family. Thank you to my own family and our shared origin story. As always, to Reed and Zaza, the West Works Writers Co-op.